D1623924

SUCKERPUNCH

SUCKERPUNCH

DAVID HERNANDEZ

HARPER TEEN
An Imprint of HarperCollins Publishers

For Lisa

HarperTeen is an imprint of HarperCollins Publishers.

Suckerpunch
Copyright © 2008 by David Hernandez

www.harperteen.com

Library of Congress Cataloging-in-Publication Data is available.
Hernandez, David, date.
    Suckerpunch / David Hernandez.— 1st ed.
        p.   cm.
    Summary: Shy, seventeen-year-old Marcus and his sixteen-year-old
brother, Enrique, accompanied by two friends, drive from their home in
Southern California to Monterey to confront the abusive father who
walked out a year earlier, and who now wants to return home.
    ISBN 978-0-06-117330-1 (trade bdg.)
    ISBN 978-0-06-117331-8 (lib. bdg.)
    [1. Child abuse—Fiction. 2. Brothers—Fiction. 3. Fathers and sons—
Fiction. 4. Drug abuse—Fiction. 5. Family life—California—Fiction. 6.
Hispanic-Americans—Fiction. 7. California—Fiction.] I. Title. II. Title:
Suckerpunch.
PZ7.H43174Suc 2008   2007024182
[Fic]—dc22   CIP
                                                                  AC

Typography by Larissa Lawrynenko
10 11 12 13   CG/RRDB   10 9 8 7 6 5 4
❖
First Edition

ACKNOWLEDGMENTS

I am indebted to my wife, Lisa Glatt, for encouraging me to write this book and for her invaluable help throughout the process. I am grateful to my parents, James and Nancy Hernandez, for their bottomless love and support. Fistbumps to Ernie Liang for giving a hoot (even though he dumped an earlier version of the manuscript in Hong Kong) and to Alex Lemon for Catface, Haterade, and finite wisdom. Many thanks to my brilliant editor, Lauren Velevis, for her wonderful ideas and sharp eyes, Michael Stearns, and everyone at HarperCollins. And finally, a big thank-you to the good people at Writers House, especially my enthusiastic and dedicated agent, Steven Malk.

1

AT THE FUNERAL FOR Oliver's father I daydreamed about killing my own. I'd come at him with a switchblade while he was in the garage, the table saw whirring in his hand as it chewed through a 4x4. I'd come at him with a hammer. I'd come at him with a baseball bat, his head splitting open like rotten fruit. With stealth I'd come at him, his back always turned, the way he finally turned his back on us early one morning and drove off to who-knows-where.

The minister had a comb-over and silver-rimmed glasses. His face was pink as a slice of ham and his lips were thin, almost nonexistent. With his thin lips he spoke highly of Mr. Thompson—what a great father he was to his son, what a great husband—and I remember thinking, *How the hell would you know? Did you have a hidden camera in their bedroom and watch him make Mrs. Thompson come? Were you there when Oliver wiped out on his bike and Mr. Thompson sprayed Bactine on his knee, then ruffled his hair and called him a tough guy even though Oliver was bawling his eyes out?*

I looked over at Oliver, who wasn't bawling now. He wore a white button-down shirt, black slacks and shoes. He had the pamphlet with his father's face on the cover rolled up into a paper baton. He slowly turned toward me, his dilated pupils large as dimes, then turned back to the minister, who was going on and on about Jesus and the valley of darkness and the glory of the Lord Almighty.

Mrs. Thompson wore a black veil and barely moved.

There is nothing more precious than life, the minister said, than to do the will of God. And the only thing more powerful than death is the supreme power of Jesus.

I imagined Jesus with lightning bolts zigzagging out

from his palms. I imagined one of those bolts striking my dad through his chest, his eyes rolling back, skin smoldering and foam bubbling out of his mouth. I imagined my dad in the mahogany casket instead of Mr. Thompson.

After the service, Oliver wanted to know what I had planned for the evening. Even though the sun was right on his face, his pupils were still huge.

I've got nothing going on, I said.

Want to get wasted?

Sure.

My dad left behind a lot of booze.

How's your mom doing?

She's on Valium. Want any?

Before I could answer, Mrs. Thompson came out of the wooden doors of the church and walked up to Oliver.

I know you're still angry, she said, her voice quivering, watered down. You don't have to come to the burial if you don't want to.

I don't want to, Oliver said.

You sure?

I'm sure.

It's something you might regret later on when—

I won't regret it, he said, cutting her off.

Fine, she said.

Mrs. Thompson glanced at me. Sometimes when I beat off I thought of her sucking me. Now she was standing before me, wrecked. The black roses sewn to her veil looked like flies on a window screen.

I'm sorry for your loss, I said, which sounded stupid after I said it. As if she'd misplaced her husband. As if he were wedged between the couch cushions. As if she'd opened her purse and Mr. Thompson slipped out and fell through the bars of a grate, and all she could do was watch him glinting down there at the bottom.

What actually happened was he walked down to the basement with an orange extension cord and hanged himself.

You're a good boy, Marcus, Mrs. Thompson said to me. Then she squeezed Oliver's arm lightly and then headed toward the inky black car that waited to take her to the cemetery. She climbed into the backseat and closed the door, her face hidden behind the tinted window reflecting the fat white clouds sailing above us.

So what time should I pick you up tonight? Oliver wanted to know.

Anytime after eight, I said. Honk when you get to my house.

My horn stopped working.

Rev your engine then.

All right.

More people spilled out from the church and down the concrete steps. An elderly woman with a back curved like an awning. A man with an eye patch, tapping a cigarette out from a pack. This little girl in a powder blue dress, holding her father's hand.

Oliver and I stood there in our black clothes, watching. I didn't know what to say. I looked over at Oliver, at his large pupils.

What happens when you try to honk? I finally said.

Nothing happens, he answered. A small wind played with a piece of hair that had fallen across his forehead. Just silence, he said.

My home was a two-story house with cream siding and a shrub at the entrance that my mom kept clipping into some dumb animal. One month it was a cow, a couple months later it was a grizzly bear, and sometimes I didn't know what it was, a creature half horse and half antelope. The front door of our house was chocolate brown, as was the roof, where a glow-in-the-dark Frisbee was stuck on the shingles, as if someone had gone up there to eat dinner and left their plate behind. My home had a swimming pool and a giant lemon tree sagging with fruit. It had four bedrooms and a chandelier dangling over the foyer like a garish earring.

The day of the funeral, I came home and found Enrique standing in his room with his head bowed, his palms pressed flat against the wall. Between his hands there was a hole, the knuckles of his right hand were dusted with drywall. What? he said, even though I hadn't said anything. He was sixteen then, one year younger than me.

You okay?

Yeah.

What happened?

Nothing.

It doesn't look like nothing happened.

I was just pissed, that's all.

And felt like punching the wall, I said, finishing his sentence.

Right.

That's really smart.

Enrique picked up a paper clip from his desk and began straightening it out.

You still on a hundred? I asked him.

I've been breaking them in half.

Don't break them, I said. Stay on a hundred.

They make me drowsy.

Better to be drowsy than to do something stupid like *that*, I said, pointing at the wall, the hole like a yawning mouth. How long have you been on fifty? I wanted to know.

About two weeks.

Go back on a hundred, I said.

Okay, okay.

My dad always said Enrique didn't need antidepressants, that he just needed to snap out of it. He said the psychiatrist was too expensive and the money could be spent on fixing up the house instead, to build a deck in the backyard, to get shingles on the roof like the O'Donnell house down the street. *He's a tough kid,* my dad said. *He could tough it out.*

I pointed at the hole in the wall. Mom's gonna shit when she sees that, I said.

She won't see it, he said.

Enrique unpinned his sports calendar and moved it over the hole. It was May 2005. Above the row of days —half of them already X'd out—was a photograph of a water-skier flying across a lake, leaning as he turned, a clear fan of water spreading out behind him.

There, he said.

The garage door grumbled open, then our mom shouted for us. Marcus, Enrique, *¡ayúdame!*

I looked at my little brother. Go fix up your hand before Mom sees it.

If this had happened a year earlier, I would've said *Go fix up your hand before Dad sees it.* He would've pummeled Enrique had he seen the hole. He would've left Enrique bruised and speechless.

I found my mom in the kitchen, holding two plump bags of groceries. My mom was a short woman with tea-colored skin. She had brown hair flecked with gray that she cut short and brushed away from her face. How did it go at the funeral? she asked.

Boring as shit, I said, grabbing one of the grocery bags from her arms.

Marcus.

Well, it was.

That poor boy.

Oliver'll be all right, I said, which I half believed. The other half saw him getting more and more messed up. The other half saw him swallowing Valium with beer and then lighting up.

The market was so crowded today, my mom said. And there were only two checkout lines open. Why do they do that?

You should've let me go, I said.

You were at a funeral.

I could've gone last night.

You don't know what we need, she said.

Seeing my own mom there made me think of Mrs. Thompson's sad eyes behind the mesh of her veil.

I know how to read a grocery list, I said, making room in the refrigerator for the gallon of milk.

You don't know where everything is, my mom said. Do you know where the tuna is? It's not easy finding the tuna.

Mom, I'm not an idiot.

Yes, I know.

From now on I'll go, I said.

Okay. My mom turned around to get the other groceries from the car. I stopped her.

Let me, I said. I'll do the rest.

She clapped my cheeks softly between her hands. Look at this handsome face, she said, then squeezed my arm lightly the way Mrs. Thompson had squeezed Oliver's.

Later that night, Oliver parked at the end of Edgefield Avenue and we climbed out of his truck and up the concrete steps that opened up to our school, the fenced-in football field and aluminum bleachers. Above the gymnasium was the bitten fingernail of the moon, giving us just a teaspoon of light. A cricket squeaked and squeaked in the grass. Oliver had on the same pair of black pants he'd worn to the funeral but had changed his shirt into one he found at a thrift store—a gray-striped mechanic's shirt with *Sergio* embroidered in blue thread on the name patch.

He opened the paper bag he carried with him and

pulled out a tiny bottle and handed it to me.

What the hell's this? I asked.

Cisco, he said. My dad had a stash of them in the cupboard.

Oliver took out his bottle before he balled up the paper bag and tossed it into the night.

How am I supposed to get bombed on this little thing? I said.

Trust me, you will, he said. It's bum wine. Read the label.

I did. It said Black Cherry. It said the bottle served four and that it was not a cooler. It said Formaldehyde.

Holy shit, it's got formaldehyde in it, I said.

I know.

Don't they use that for embalming?

I think so, Oliver said. Cheers, Nub.

We clinked our tiny bottles.

When I was eleven my right index finger was severed at the second knuckle, so my friends called me Nub. After booze or drugs or both, they called me whatever their clouded minds could dream up, their voices slurred and far away like a cassette tape warped by heat. *Hey, Freak Show*, they would say. *What's up,*

Nine? they'd ask, smiles pushing up their rubbery faces. This is what they called me, my friends. Never just Marcus.

I took a swig and shivered. It was as if I'd swallowed lightning.

Have you drawn anything lately? Oliver wanted to know.

Nah, I said, which wasn't true. Before he'd picked me up I was in my bedroom sketching Mrs. Thompson's profile, how the veil draped around her face. I drew the little black flowers. Underneath her chin I crosshatched with a charcoal pencil and then dragged the black down with the side of my thumb.

My mom always encouraged me to draw. She wanted me to graduate from high school and focus on art in college. Sometimes she'd call me a famous artist's name instead of Marcus. As in, *Hey, Michelangelo, what do you want for dinner?* or *Please take out the trash, Picasso.* My dad was just as supportive of my art, but he showed it differently than Mom. He was an architect and said I drew better than he did when he was my age. *The shading is perfect, mijo,* he used to say. Sometimes when I drew now, I wondered if my pencil was what saved me from my dad. The thought alone was enough to make me close my sketchbook.

I know I should've done something the first time I saw my dad hit Enrique. I should've put a hand on my dad's shoulder and said, *Stop it* or *That's enough* or *He's just a kid.* Instead, I quaked in the corner of the living room with my hands pressed to my ears, just a kid myself.

Draw me something, Oliver said, lifting the bottle to his lips and taking a sip.

Like what?

I don't know. Draw me a chick, or a gun. Draw me a car. Anything.

How about a chick in a car with a gun?

Yeah, Oliver said, and laughed, which was pretty amazing considering that he'd been at his father's funeral seven hours earlier. I wanted to ask him why his father killed himself. I wanted him to tell me without me having to ask, but I figured he'd tell me if he wanted me to know.

He seemed like a kind man, Oliver's father. It didn't make sense that he did what he did, the way it didn't make sense that my own dad would beat Enrique for the dumbest things. Like the day he jumped from his lime green sofa chair when he heard the lawn mower go over the rock, the pop and guttural rattle of the whirling blade. He swung open the front door and made a beeline toward Enrique, who was crouched on the grass beside the upended mower, examining its mechanics. He shot past my mom, who was trimming the hedge. I was on the driveway, juggling a soccer ball from my left foot to my right and back to my left, but stopped when I saw my dad charging. *I think we can fix it,* Enrique said just before Dad backhanded him, before the blood came to his lips. My dad called him an idiot, he called him incompetent. *It was a damn accident,* Enrique said. My dad backhanded him again and pushed the mower into the garage and lifted it onto his workbench. My mom went inside the house covering her mouth and left her shears by the hedge, a grizzly bear that needed more clipping around the snout.

Oliver and I drank and shivered, drank and shivered. The blocky silhouette of our school stood in the distance, a cutout against the blue-black of the evening. Our junior year was almost over and people were already asking us, What are you doing after high school? We didn't know the answer, nor did we like the options we were left with—work or college. We wanted a third option, something less painful and mundane.

You hear that? Oliver said. His head was cocked.

What?

Listen.

All I hear is that damn cricket, I said.

No, *listen*.

Then I heard it, coming from the darkness of the football field: A girl was moaning in pleasure.

Oh, shit, I said. Is that what I think it is?

We sat still and didn't move so that we could hear better. For a few seconds the girl's moaning was barely audible, like a neighbor's television at night, and then the wind would carry her cries to our ears, clear as anything.

Touchdown, Oliver said.

Let's sneak up on them.

And do what?

Give him some pointers, I said. Penalize him for

illegal use of the hands.

Nah, Oliver said, taking a swig from his bottle.

Come on, I persisted.

How are *you* going to give *anyone* pointers?

Man, I get laid.

Sure you do, Nub, he said, smirking.

Forget it, I said. I took a nip and again my body quivered, hoping Oliver couldn't read the history of my sex life on my face, which consisted of only one chapter: The Handjob of 2003. In it, a girl named Camille Dawson—a drunk and pudgy-faced girl—dropped on the couch beside me and said, *Are you Nub?* I told her that's what my friends call me but that she could call me Marcus. Five Heinekens later and we were in one of the bedrooms, away from the party. I unzipped my jeans and she put her hand down around me and pulled and pulled until I squirted all over the carpet. She said, *Whoa, Jesus,* and began to laugh. She wouldn't stop laughing so I zipped up and left, my legs all jellylike as I walked down the hallway and across the living room and into the backyard, where a small crowd had gathered by the swimming pool to watch Britt Souza, fully clothed, do a backflip from the diving board, the water leaping around him like a turquoise flower.

I was nothing like Enrique, who had three girl-friends during his freshman year. He was confident without being arrogant, charming without sounding fake. My little brother had all the moves. I had one: a quick smile followed by a downward gaze at my shoes.

I took another nip from my bottle and thought about this girl I'd seen that morning at Tempo Records before driving over to the funeral. She had a pierced nose and her hair was dyed black. Her lipstick was the color of smashed cranberries. She was click-ing through the CDs one by one, her fingernails painted metallic blue. I wondered what color her panties were, and it wasn't long before my mind had her bent over the CDs and I was inside her, the sound of her whimpering in rhythm with the drumbeat thumping from the store's speakers, and on her back the silk-screened names of every city the Pixies played on their reunion tour.

By the time Oliver and I finished our Ciscos the field was quiet again. I was more than buzzed and so was Oliver. The ground tilted away from me like the floor of a boat in choppy water.

We hopped into his truck and tore down the road, the streetlights dazzling the windshield, the stereo cranked and blaring the primal drums and noisy guitars we loved so much.

Slow down, dude, I yelled over the music.

I'm all right, he yelled back.

Oliver peeled around a turn and the truck hydroplaned over a puddle and suddenly we were fishtailing, the tires spinning below us. Before Oliver turned the wheel in the direction of the skid and had control of his truck again, we were facing a one-story house, all lit up by the headlights. For a moment I could see through the bay window and into the house, the L-shaped couch where a family sat watching television. I could see the mother. I could see the son and the daughter. And I could see the father, his wife-beater shirt and thinning hair, his thick-rimmed glasses as he turned toward the window, wondering about the light.

2

IT WAS EARLY JULY—summer break. The humidity that night was a thin layer of gel on my skin. We were crouched behind a green Dumpster in the Travelodge parking lot, relieved to be out of school, ready to get inside and get wasted. From the Dumpster's shadow, my friends and I watched Darren Glick talk to the manager, a silent movie framed by the motel's office window. Oliver stood beside me, rattling the bag of pills he kept in his jean pocket. Britt was making that noise he always made with his mouth that sounded like a giant mosquito was flying nearby.

A stench like hydrogen sulfide emanated from the open lid of the Dumpster.

That reeks, I said.

It smells like Oliver, don't it, Nub? Britt said.

It smells like your mom, Oliver said.

It smells like your mom's snatch.

It smells like your dad's breath after he's given a skunk a rim job.

Under different circumstances—say it was April, the month before Oliver's father killed himself—Britt would've shot back with something equally offensive about his father. The best he could do was redirect an insult back toward Oliver: It smells like your dick after a night alone at the stables.

It was no wonder that none of us had a girlfriend. Our mouths were as filthy as the Dumpster we were crouched behind.

Headlights from a car illuminated our shirts and faces for the briefest moment, shards of broken glass gleamed at our feet.

The brown and beige motel was at the edge of Cerritos, the town where we lived and stole and vandalized, whether it was the record store (CDs Frisbeed over the metal detector) or the movie theater (a coffee can full of marbles poured out in the darkness, rolling toward the screen) or the grotesque monstrosity of the mall (parked car after parked car scraped with fisted keys) or the public library (a box of detergent dumped in the three-tiered fountain until it was frothing over) or Liberty Park (loaded on the slide, loaded on the swings, loaded on the spin ride as the oatmeal of someone's vomit flew out of his mouth) or the high school we hoped to graduate from (an inflated blow-up doll duct-taped hip to hip to the bronze Trojan sculpture that stood at the school's entrance).

Of the four in our group, I was the youngest by two months. If you saw us all lined up, you'd think I was even younger, fourteen and not seventeen. I had a baby face. After I took a shower I'd lean close to the mirror and inspect my chin, searching for one god-damn hair. My face was smooth, butterscotch brown.

Darren was the only one with a fake ID. He had graduated from our high school the month before. Barely. His whiskered face and husky voice added a good five years to his actual age. His voice was like my dad's voice, and whenever he shouted out one of my nicknames in the hallway at school, part of me flinched, the part that worried about my dad coming back to beat up my little brother for anything all over again. Like the cranberry juice he spilled that led to a cranberry bruise on his back, or that afternoon Enrique ruined the lawn mower when he pushed it over a rock, or the day he muddied the carpet with his footprints. The ladder he carried and the ceiling he scratched. The wooden bat and the aquarium in the living room he smacked on the backswing, the fish clueless as a steady stream of salt water dribbled out from a jagged crack.

Our dad left us early in the morning on July 5, 2004. The day before there was a big fight in the kitchen—he knocked three teeth out of Enrique's mouth. His good-bye note was handwritten on a piece of lined paper and stuck to the refrigerator with a watermelon magnet. The note read: *I'm leaving. Don't look for me.* He left at dawn with the sidewalks smudged with black powder and the smoky scent of fireworks still in the air. He backed his car out of the garage and left, the dark purple sky above him going lavender. I could see him clicking on the radio. I'm sure he took the 5. He was miles away when Enrique shook me awake. Asshole's gone, he said.

I noticed that the manager of the Travelodge looked like my dad. He was a large man with a large gut. He was shaped like a pear. My dad's hands were lined with scars from the years of construction work he did during his twenties. He had narrow wrists like a woman's but his arms were muscled and stretched the sleeves of his T-shirts. His hair was wavy and as black as a raven's wing and he had a mole the size of a chocolate chip on the side of his nose. His eyes were mud brown with flecks of gold. Whenever he screamed, the gold flecks of his eyes would shine.

I hadn't seen my dad in a year, but I was always bumping into someone who reminded me of him. A shoe salesman. The new janitor at school. Some stranger sitting at a bus stop wearing wraparound shades. And now the manager at the Travelodge.

He rubbed his chin and said something to Darren. Darren shook his head and the manager rubbed his chin again.

Give him a damn room already, Britt said.

And just like that, as if he'd heard Britt's plea, the manager turned to the back wall and pulled a key down from its wooden peg.

Once Darren opened the door, we moved quickly inside as if we were a SWAT team. The room had sea foam green carpet and mauve drapes and floral wallpaper. There was a single king-size bed, a cheap nightstand, a lamp with a conical lampshade, a yellow love seat, and a color TV atop a dresser.

Classy, Oliver said.

Britt sprinted toward the bed and launched his body, twisting midair and landing on his back, the blond wood headboard smacking against the wall.

Idiot, Darren said. He flipped open his cell phone and began making some calls.

I hit the light switch in the bathroom. A dish of dried flowers beside the sink perfumed the air with cinnamon. A sign Scotch-taped above the towel rack said: DO NOT TAKE THE TOWELS. If the manager knew what kind of people we were, he'd have signs taped all over our room. DO NOT TAKE THE BLOW-DRYER. DO NOT TAKE THE TELEPHONE. DO NOT TAKE THE DIGITAL CLOCK RADIO. DO NOT TAKE THE COFFEEMAKER. DO NOT TAKE THE IRON OR THE IRONING BOARD. DO NOT TAKE THE TELEVISION.

Oliver stood beside me and shook his Ziploc of

pills. They were white and looked like aspirin. My mom's stash, he said. You want one?

What is it?

Valium.

Nah, I said. What else you got?

Oliver pulled from his wallet a small sheet that was perforated into little squares. Bart Simpson's spiked and yellow head was printed on each one. Acid, Oliver said. My uncle from San Francisco gave these to me before the funeral.

I've never done acid before, I said. I examined the sheet, turning it over. What if I have a bad trip?

It happens sometimes, he said. But usually not, he added.

I thought about it. One of my favorite artists was Salvador Dalí and I imagined my world would look something like one of his paintings, full of melting clocks and fluffy clouds and tall elephants with legs like mosquitoes. I tore off one of the square tabs. What about you? I asked.

I already swallowed a couple of these, Oliver said, shaking the plastic Baggie.

You're going to black out.

Probably.

How 'bout Britt?

He's got that Afghan weed.

Fuckin' stoner.

He's a Bongoloid.

Good one, I said. I placed the paper blotter on my tongue as if I were licking a tiny postage stamp. I pictured a little man walking out of his miniature house, opening his tin mailbox, and finding my letter, my name so small in the upper left-hand corner it could be anyone's name.

About my finger.

I was eleven, like I said before. I was a boy on Rollerblades, a skinny kid with daredevil blood. Sidewalk under my wheels and the wind in my face. I had the sound of my dad's angry voice from the night before looping in my ear, shouting at Enrique that he was *useless*, branding the word into his skull.

I had a ramp I made with a rectangle of plywood propped on a cinder block. Enrique was my audience. He sat cross-legged on the grass and cheered, *Go, go, go!*

Midair, I looked down and saw the sidewalk's history: the spidery cracks, a wad of gum's fat period, the faded chalk lines of hopscotch. I flew over my handprint from when the concrete was still wet and the construction workers were done for the day. When I landed, I landed perfectly with my arms stretched out like the wings of a plane.

Suddenly there was a small rock under my wheel and I lost my balance. I swerved to the right and tipped, the ground rushing toward me. I grabbed on to the brick wall that separated our driveway from the Murphys' front yard. There was the grating sound of a single brick loosening, coming off that wall like a tooth. The brick fell toward my other hand, splayed on the driveway.

Then I blacked out.

When the world came back to me, I was in the hospital with my right hand bandaged up. It looked like a skinny man wearing a turban. My parents were in the room and quietly arguing, full of hisses.

Christ, Nora, my dad said. How could you be so stupid?

There was blood everywhere, my mom said. He was

out cold, Enrique was crying. I wanted to get him to the hospital as fast as possible.

You didn't think to see where all the blood was coming from? my dad asked. You didn't see his damn finger lying there on the ground?

Don't you dare blame me for this, too.

Who then? *Who?* he said.

Enrique sat quietly by himself in a corner chair, playing with his Game Boy. He had that bored demeanor of a child who'd seen his parents argue a hundred times before.

Story goes that after the accident, Enrique had run into the house and called my mom, who was making a pot roast for dinner. Story goes she panicked when she saw me lying there, when she saw all the blood. Story goes Enrique had to help her carry me into the station wagon. When they pulled out of the driveway, Mom left the front door wide open, the scent of beef and carrots and onions drifting into the street.

Sure I was upset, losing my finger and all, but I knew from then on I'd always get my way with my guilt-ridden mother. Anything I wanted.

Mom, can I have fifty bucks?

Yes, dear.

Mom, can I borrow your kitchen knife?

Yes, dear.

Mom, can I smoke a joint and piss on that fancy rug in the living room?

Yes, dear.

While I was lying there in the hospital bed, my father went looking for my severed finger. This brought me some satisfaction, imagining him on the driveway, tie loosened, searching for my lost digit and in the end finding only a small red pool.

I have this theory about what happened to my finger. Our street was always mobbed with crows. By late afternoon you could hear them making a racket outside, squawking as if they were on fire. I'm almost certain that one of them must've picked up my finger. I could see the crow now, swooping down and gliding to our driveway, shuffling toward the blood, then taking off with my finger at the end of its beak, pointing at the sky.

In our motel room at the Travelodge I was watching bodies undulate on the television screen. They were rainbowed and speckled with static and swayed as if underwater, swimming in and out of a surface that rippled and waved. The bodies, the two that I could make out, were naked.

Is that a porno? Oliver wanted to know.

Who brought roses? I said. I smell roses.

No one brought roses. You're tripping.

You don't smell any roses?

Oliver walked past the television and smeared its colors, which trailed behind him like comet dust.

There was a knock and Darren pushed the drapes to the side before opening the door. It was Beth Guzman and the girl I'd seen two months ago at Tempo Records, her hair now green. At the record store it had been black, a black so dark it turned blue when she stood by the store's window, sunlit and plastered with band stickers. Now I was tripping and the stud on her nose winked like a star. She turned her head and her hair was green fire swelling. She didn't seem too concerned about it.

Hey, Marcus, Beth said.

Call him Nub, Britt said.

I'm not calling him that.

But he has one.

I raised my hand. I mostly did this for the green-haired girl. I closed one eye so that she occupied the space where the rest of my finger should have been.

I'm Ashley, she said.

Hi, I said, and laughed because my hand was already up, waving hello.

The night went like this: I sat on the edge of the bed and watched the door close and open and then someone else stood in the doorway. It could've been the same person, changing his or her own face, but the room began to fill so I knew that wasn't possible. The scent of roses drifted in and out. Beer cans hissed open, the sound of bottle rockets taking off. The bodies warbled on the screen. Someone jumped on or off the bed and the mattress bucked underneath me. One voice braided with another voice. When someone laughed, the room exploded with pink light.

Ashley walked past the television screen and the colors followed her.

You're killing me, I said.

Excuse me? she said, turning toward me.

I'm dying here, looking at you.

You're wasted.

You're still killing me.

Thanks.

Your hair was on fire when you got here and now it's dripping lava.

Like I said, she said, and stepped into the bathroom.

In the corner of the room, Beth was topless and straddling some guy sitting on the yellow love seat. His hands were a pair of tarantulas that slowly crawled up her naked back.

Yo, Freak Show, Britt said. Oliver's out, man.

At first I thought he was talking to me in code, but then I looked where Britt was looking and saw Oliver slumped in the corner, the side of his head pressed against the nightstand as if he were listening to something inside one of the drawers. Harsh light from the toppled lamp washed out his face.

Oh, I said.

There was fierce banging at the door and everyone shut up and looked at one another.

Hide, Darren said. *Hide*, you fucks.

We all scooted into the bathroom, shushing one

another. A big guy everyone called Tower carried Oliver and sat him on the toilet. Six people stood in the bathtub. Britt's eyes were hooded and glossy red. Ashley winked at me, her hair dripping emerald again onto her shoulders. The door closed and someone hit the lights.

Darren's voice was muffled as he tried to convince the manager he was alone.

Hey, Oliver said. Are my eyes open?

Shut up, someone whispered.

I can't *see*.

Dipshit, the lights are *off*.

Oliver started sobbing. A drunk girl who obviously didn't know about Oliver's dad started to giggle, a bell pinging inside my ears. I reached my hand out toward where Ashley had stood before the lights went out and grabbed air. The scent of roses was stronger, as if someone were standing right beside me holding a bouquet. A spotted shark glided out of the darkness with a face like my dad's. Oh shit, I said, flinching. The shark snapped at me and I flinched again, needles bristled on my arm. I was having a bad trip and there was nothing I could do about it. It was like falling off a high-rise building and telling yourself *I don't want to fall anymore*. You just had to wait until you hit the bottom.

Get out, get out, the manager yelled from behind the door. *I call the cops.*

Some of us were drunk. Some of us were stoned. Some of us were on acid and had an aurora borealis in our head. But we were all on the same leaky boat in that motel bathroom, too dark to see where we were going, too smashed to even care.

3

WHEN WE WERE KIDS, my dad would twist a lemon off its branch and toss it into the swimming pool. The first one to grab it would get a dollar. Enrique and I would jump in and paddle furiously toward the yellow fruit, a little sun bobbing on the waves. I'd grab the lemon first or Enrique would and then my dad would reach into his back pocket and pull out his wallet. He'd hand me or Enrique a dollar bill and one of us got to feel rich for a day.

My dad worked long hours in a tall office building in Culver City. Sometimes he came home early with cardboard tubes of floor plans under his arm. In his office at our house there were blueprints thumbtacked to the walls, the bones of a gymnasium or bridge. His desk had a transparent T-square attached to the side that slid up and down. He used the lopsided coffee mug I made in kindergarten to hold his pencils. He had a snow globe paperweight, a miniature cabin surrounded by a dome of glass. Beside the tiny pyramid of logs, a man leaned on his axe. *That*, he told me once, *is me in a nutshell.*

Now it was my mom who had to work, who drove off to waitress at this fancy Thai restaurant called the Palace, who came home tired and smelling of spices—lemongrass and curry and tamarind. If she wasn't too exhausted, she sometimes made us empanadas for dinner and rolled out the dough right on the kitchen counter.

It was a warm July evening and we sat down for dinner, the three of us, at a table designed for four. Where the bulk of my dad used to be was now an unobstructed view of the backyard, the pool's diving board and lemon tree.

The empanadas glistened on a platter. Some were filled with ground beef, onions, raisins, bits of egg. Some only had mozzarella cheese. When we sank our teeth into them, we didn't know what we were getting.

Damn, I said. These are good, Mom.

It's been a while, huh?

You should make them more often.

It's a lot of work, Marcus.

Yeah, well, I said, then scratched my chin with my stubby finger.

Enrique took a large bite from his empanada and the melted cheese stretched from his mouth like a rubber band. *Hot, hot,* he said, his mouth wide open.

My God, Enrique, my mom said. What happened to your hand?

We all looked at Enrique's hand resting beside his plate, the pink and swollen knuckles.

Oh, he said, pausing. I dropped a dumbbell on it.

Enrique was always doing curls then—while he watched television, while he talked on the phone, five sets for each arm before bed. Still, I could tell that he was lying and imagined he'd punched the wall again, that he had to find something to tack over it besides his calendar.

Did you put ice on it? my mom asked.

No.

After you finish dinner, I want you to put some ice on it.

Okay, he said, and glanced over at me before wiping his lips with a napkin.

We heard our neighbor behind us then. The father. He barked at his wife or his kids. A door slammed and then a threat, something about removing the hinges off the door. Then the pounding of manual labor, as if he was actually following through on his threat.

Now *that* family has problems, I said.

He should leave, too, Enrique added.

My mom clicked her tongue and shook her head and she reached for an empanada and bit into the corner. A ribbon of steam rose from the opening as if a little fire had been put out.

I looked at the empty seat where my dad once sat, remembering when he pointed his fork at Enrique. *Eat your broccoli*, he said. *Now*. When Enrique didn't move, my dad stood and grabbed him by the neck, forcing him toward the only thing left on his plate, the little green trees of my mom's favorite vegetable. *Get off me!* Enrique shouted. My dad let go of his neck and sat back down, his face flushed. *Look what you make me do,* he said. My mom covered her mouth with her hand and I just sat there quietly at the table, wondering what my little brother would make him do next.

Enrique looked at his watch. Shit, I'm late.

Language, my mom said.

Where are you going? I wanted to know.

Movies. Ashley wants to see that piece of shit with Johnny Depp.

My *ears,* my mom said, caging her ears with her hands.

Sorry, sorry. She wants to see that piece of feces with Johnny Depp.

That's better.

Ashley who? I said.

Ashley Mahoney. You know, Beth's friend. She said she met you at a party a couple weeks ago?

The night at the motel came back to me. Oliver's Valium Baggie. The acid, the roses. Ashley's green hair moving like sea life. All of us crammed in that darkened bathroom.

Oh yeah, I said. *Ashley.*

What about your hand? my mom said.

I'll put ice on it later.

Enrique stood up from the table. My mom and I watched him rinse his plate at the sink, the muscles of his forearm as his hand circled underneath the faucet. Enrique had grown quite a lot over the year. He was taller and his shoulders were wider. His voice was more husky, a voice on its way to sounding like Dad's. Much to Mom's disapproval, he began to grow out his coffee brown hair, which framed his face. The anti-depressants had added some plump to his cheeks. There was even stubble on his chin. And his eyes. All we had to do was look at his eyes to know that he wasn't a boy anymore. Watching him rinse his plate, I felt like I was the younger brother.

Once Enrique was out of the house, I walked into his room and noticed immediately the Radiohead poster that was now taped on the wall beside the cal-endar. With my fingertip, I tapped around the poster until it buckled inward, warping Thom Yorke's face. I knew it.

Later that evening, my mom stood in the doorway of my bedroom. I was on my bed with my back against the wall, knees bent with my sketchbook resting on my thighs. I was drawing a girl holding a beer bottle, a girl with black boots sitting cross-legged. I was drawing the rivers of her hair. I was drawing Ashley.

Can I see, Picasso? my mom asked.

I'll show you when I'm finished.

You know, you can take some art classes at the junior college. You don't have to wait until you graduate from high school.

Don't start, I said.

Marcus, I worry about you, she said. You need to start thinking about your future, what you want to do with your life. You need to start thinking about how you're going to make money.

Okay, got it, I said. My future, my life. I'll start thinking about it now. I held my chin with one hand and looked upward, my tongue poking out from the corner of my mouth.

Don't be a smart aleck, she said, turning away from the doorway. Maybe I should send you to the Army.

They won't have me.

Why not? she hollered from the end of the hallway.

Because I don't have a trigger finger, I hollered back.

I clicked on the television and watched the news for a while. Whenever my dad watched the news, he would insert his opinion between sips from his beer. *It's about time we invaded Iraq.* Sip. *If my neighbor did that, I'd punch his lights out.* Sip. *Everyone is shooting everyone these days.* Sip. *That's what she gets for leaving her baby in the car.* Sip. *The world is going to hell in a handbasket.* Sip. *No one could beat the Yankees.*

The anchorwoman said the botched terrorist attack in London was most likely attempted by the same group who were behind the last bombings. This time the bombs failed to explode correctly. I thought about how dumb the terrorists must've felt and imagined them pointing fingers at one another. I thought about the funeral and the tiny flowers on Mrs. Thompson's veil. I thought about banging the anchorwoman, who had a brown helmet of hair and a pug nose but still looked hot to me, what with her big blue eyes and full lips. Then I thought about Ashley sitting beside my brother at the movies, sharing a tub of buttered popcorn. The whole thing made me ill.

That night I dreamed I was in our swimming pool, surrounded by hundreds of lemons. They knocked against my shoulders and chest. I could smell their fragrant yellow skin. Beside the empty lemon tree, my dad stood in a bright blue Hawaiian shirt. A dollar per lemon, he said. So *this* was how I was going to make money, I thought. And then another thought: *Where's Enrique?* I looked at my dad. He shrugged his shoulders, his arms now gone, his empty sleeves blue flags waving at his sides.

I was slow-footed and stoned at the market with a Spoon album on my iPod. The joint was Britt's, half of it smoked in the parking lot before I wet my fingers and pinched the end.

I pushed the shopping cart up and down the aisles, my face numb. Everything looked so good. The bananas and the peaches looked good. The garlic-flavored croutons, the jars of green olives, the cans of pinto beans. Even the filleted salmon on ice looked tasty.

There were eleven items on the grocery list, scrawled in my mom's neat handwriting: milk, eggs, orange juice, lettuce, Raisin Bran, ground beef, mozzarella cheese, tuna, paper towels, razors (for

Enrique), and peanut butter.

Someone tapped my shoulder and I turned around. It was Mrs. Thompson, dressed in jeans and a large sweatshirt, her hair in a messy ponytail. I pulled the earphones off and let the little speakers buzz on my stomach.

Hi, I said.

Hello, Marcus. I just wanted to thank you for coming to the funeral. It meant a lot to Oliver.

He'd do the same for me, I said, wondering how bloodshot my eyes looked, if she could smell the weed on my clothes.

Yes, he would.

How are you doing?

Not so good, she said, and smiled weakly. Her eyes got wet and I was afraid she'd lose it then, that I'd have to find a way to console her, stoned as I was, surrounded by the brightly colored boxes of cereal. I imagined the store's intercom crackling overhead: *Cleanup on aisle seven. Sobbing widow.*

I'm taking it day by day, she said.

That's the only way to take it, I said. I looked down at my shoelaces, then up at her face.

You're right. You had to do the same thing with your father.

It's better that he's gone.

Mrs. Thompson blinked.

My dad, that is, I said. I didn't want you to think —

I knew who you meant, she said.

I looked down at my laces again.

Well, she said, I'll let you get back to your shopping.

It was nice seeing you, Mrs. Thompson.

Please, she said. Call me Gloria.

Okay, I said. Gloria.

She touched my wrist before rolling her cart down the aisle. I studied her ass, her wide hips, and felt my dick getting stiff in my jeans.

I skipped the razors (for Enrique) so I could push my cart through the 10 Items or Less lane. *I couldn't find them*, I'd tell my mom. *Look, I found everything else, even the tuna.*

There was an abandoned house at the edge of Cerritos, ugly as sin — an old two-story box with olive green wood paneling, weathered down from decades of rain and sun. It was as if all the other houses said

Get the hell out and this house hobbled down South Street, up Gridley, and plopped down where no one could see it. Whenever we drove by it we wondered who lived there. Britt thought they were hillbillies. Oliver imagined a meth lab. I pictured the oldest man in America sitting by the fireplace, milky white eyes and a long gray beard, a face crosshatched with a thousand wrinkles.

We noticed there was now a NO TRESPASSING sign taped to the front door. We decided to hop the fence, Oliver and I, while Britt stayed inside his Volkswagen Bug, sucking smoke out of his glass bong.

Come on, Bongoloid, don't be such a pussy, I told him.

I'm staying here, Freak Show, he said, a white thread of smoke unspooling from his lips. He reached into the back of his jeans and slid out the starter pistol. It was black with a skinny handgrip, and at the end of the barrel there was a flat, red plastic ring. The pistol belonged to his father back when he used to referee track meets at our school and around the district. Britt thought the gun made him look tough, like a gangster or something, so he carried it with him whenever possible.

I'll keep a lookout for you guys, he said, then sneered like a thug, unaware of how ridiculous he sounded.

The backyard was more dirt than grass. There was chicken wire and a row of empty five-gallon bottles of Sparkletts. A rusted tricycle was tipped over on the patio, one of its wheels missing. Against the brick wall in the corner of the yard was an old recliner, the gray cushions stained and ripped. I thought about the morning Enrique and I carried my dad's lime green sofa chair out of the house and set it beside the trash cans. I was washing our station wagon in the driveway when the garbagemen came to pick it up. The one who emptied the trash cans held the back side of the chair with his gloved hand and shouted, *This too?* I nodded, my thumb on the hose, and in one swift motion he tossed the chair into the Dumpster as if it didn't weigh a thing. Then came the whine of hydraulics as the Dumpster rose and tilted and my dad's chair tumbled down from the sky.

Oliver peered through the sliding glass door that led to the kitchen. He made blinders with his hands to cut the glare, his forehead pressed to the glass where another NO TRESPASSING sign was taped. I heard your brother's banging that Ashley chick, he said.

Yeah, I think he is.

You let your little brother cock block you?

Man, he didn't cock block me.

Oliver turned away from the sliding glass door. You were drooling all over her at the Travelodge, he said.

How would you know? I said. You were passed out.

Look, he said, and walked over to a window that was cracked open an inch from the ledge. Oliver curled his fingers inside and lifted the window and it screeched as it slid up the frame. I bet someone's shacking here, he said, wiping his hands off on his pants.

No way, I said. This dump?

Come on, let's scope it out. Oliver hoisted himself up and pushed through the window. I followed behind him, headfirst, then swung my leg over with my knee bent.

We were standing in a bathroom with checkered tile floors, white and teal. Oliver opened the medicine cabinet, which was empty. *Damn*, he said. In the sink, two fat cockroaches were slowly swaying their antennas. The tub was all grimy as if a coal miner had just taken a bath. See, man, Oliver said, pointing at a cigarette butt in the tub. Someone's shacking here.

That doesn't mean shit, I said.

I know these things.

Five bucks. I bet you five bucks.

You're on, he said.

We walked down the hall, opening cabinets, looking for something to claim as ours. All the carpet was stripped and our footsteps on the plywood floors echoed throughout the house, bouncing off the empty walls.

Honey, I'm home, Oliver shouted, his voice in stereo.

In the living room we found a cat curled up beside the fireplace, her mangy fur the color of smoke. I crouched and held out my palm. Here, kitty, kitty, kitty, I said.

I told you, Oliver said. Now pay up.

You said *someone* is shacking here. A cat's not a someone.

Yes, it is.

It's a some*thing*.

You don't know what you're talking about, Nub.

Who flunked English and had to go to summer school?

Mrs. Connelly is a bitch, Oliver said.

Doesn't matter what she is, you still flunked.

Oliver took out his wallet and pulled out the small sheet of acid.

Get that shit away from me, I said.

Sorry about your bad trip.

Never again, man. I'd rather eat glass.

Let's get this cat wasted, he said, tearing off a tab.

Give her a Valium instead.

That's no fun. She'll just lie around.

She's going to freak out, I said. Maybe we shouldn't.

Oliver held the paper blotter out on his fingertip. The cat sniffed the tiny square of paper and then looked at him timidly. Her eyes were light blue, almost transparent. Come on, Oliver said, and just like that the cat scurried away from us and up the stairs.

I wonder who used to live here, I said.

Who cares? This could be our hangout.

Yeah, we could bring chicks here and—

And what? Oliver said, cutting me off. I bet you've got cobwebs on your dick.

Ha ha, I said. I imagined Oliver's mom pulling down my boxers, brushing the cobwebs off. I imagined her taking me inside her mouth.

We heard the cat meowing somewhere upstairs and we both stood quiet, listening. Oliver went up the stairs first, two steps at a time, and I followed behind. At the top of the stairs I turned left and Oliver went right.

In the hallway there were nails poking out from the walls, white rectangles where framed pictures used to be. They were like the ghosts of photographs.

I stepped into a small bedroom that overlooked the front of the house and saw Britt's car parked along the curb, the windows clouded with smoke. There were two silver bowls in the corner of the room, one filled with water, the other with brown pellets. On the sill was a syringe and a rubber cord.

Marcus, over here, quick, Oliver shouted.

I hurried back down the hallway, full of adrenaline.

Oliver stood in the doorway of what looked like the master bedroom. He pointed at the cat, who was sniffing at the closet. She meowed and lifted her paw and scratched the closet door.

Get out, motherfucker, Oliver said, trying to sound tough.

There was silence, a moment when nothing moved, then the closet door glided open.

The man standing there was thin and had dirty blond hair. I mean he was *really* thin. It looked like his skull was leaning against his face, pressing against his pale skin. He just stood there with his arms raised above him as if we were the police. The cat walked between his legs and curled back, stepping over his dirty sneakers.

You can put your hands down, I said, and he did.

There was a mattress on the floor pushed into the corner of the room, a tin ashtray and a spoon. He had a candle still wrapped in its clear plastic, fat and white like a tall glass of milk.

You living here? Oliver asked.

Yeah, he said. Just for a while. His voice was low and soft, almost feminine.

We just wanted to scope out the place, that's all, I said.

Hey man, you guys have anything on you? He scratched his neck, his eyes darting back and forth between Oliver and me. The cat arched her back and yawned, her face nothing but tongue and teeth.

Nuh-uh, Oliver said.

How 'bout cash? You guys got any cash? He licked the corner of his mouth. They say I'm good, he said.

Nah, that's okay, I said. I reached into my pocket and pulled out a crumpled five. Here you go, I said.

He didn't move, so I dropped the bill on his mattress and it fell like a leaf.

Thanks, he said.

No problem.

Oliver and I bailed, and before I closed the front door behind us I looked upstairs. The cat had her head poked through the bars of the banister, watching us leave.

You owe me five, Oliver said.

I just gave it to him, I said, jabbing my thumb over my shoulder. That was all I had.

Oliver tapped the driver-side window of the Volkswagen and Britt jumped in his seat, startled, then rolled down the window.

Move over, Stonehenge, Oliver said. I'm driving.

What's in there? Britt wanted to know.

Just some dude who wanted to blow us, Oliver said.

And his cat, I added.

Really? Britt's eyelids were half shut. There was confusion in his voice. He wanted to blow his cat? he asked.

You dipshit, Oliver said.

The day had nothing left for us, its pockets turned inside out. We drove around Cerritos itching for something to do. Anything. I watched Oliver's eyes in the rearview mirror. They stayed on the road. I watched the back of Britt's head swaying on the head-rest. I watched the sun, low and red, staining the clouds above the tracking houses and making them look like balls of cotton, pink with blood.

What now? I said.

I don't know, man, Oliver said. I'm just driving around.

4

I'VE SEEN ENRIQUE'S CHARM work many times at school, how his smile would trigger another to smile. A girl would put her weight on one leg or twirl a strand of hair nervously or giggle like my little brother just said the wittiest thing she'd ever heard. There was Nichole Beckman. There was Carla Avila, Tammy McIntyre, and Jodi Green. The Heekin sisters and Debbie "Lip Lock" Luckenbach. But none of them, it seemed to me, he was serious about. None until Ashley Mahoney—the first girl he brought to the house.

I'm not sure if it was Enrique's idea or my mom's to invite Ashley over for dinner, but whoever's it was, I didn't like it. I was nervous all day. Ants ran around in my stomach and my palms were two damp sponges.

I opened my closet to see if I had anything cool to wear. Nothing but jeans and band T-shirts, a pair of slacks, and a few button-down long-sleeve shirts. I pulled a plaid one from the hanger and threw it on. I rolled the sleeves up, then down, then up again. In the bathroom I wet a comb under the faucet and dragged it through my hair. It looked too neat, so I flicked the front with my fingers so a few dark strands fell across my forehead. I brushed my teeth and flossed for the first time in my life. I fidgeted with my hair some more until the doorbell rang.

By the time I came downstairs, Enrique was introducing Ashley to my mom.

It's nice to meet you, Ashley said, and shook Mom's hand.

It's good to meet you too, she said, quickly glancing at Ashley's hair, all those green waves. She held her smile still. It looked as if her top and bottom teeth were glued together.

Hey, Marcus.

Hiya, I said, sounding like a dork.

Ashley lifted her nose and sniffed. That smells good, Mrs. Mendoza, whatever you're making.

Carbonada, Enrique said.

It's an old family recipe, my mom added. I hope you like it.

I'm sure I will, she said.

We stood around, the four of us. There was an awkward pause full of head nodding and smiles.

Shall we sit down? my mom finally said.

I took my usual spot at the table. Enrique sat where our dad used to sit and it was strange seeing him there, filling up that space. Ashley sat between us. Her hair smelled like apples. Under the table I wiped my palms on my jeans while my heart galloped inside my chest.

I hope you're not a vegetarian, my mom said as she set a bowl of beef stew in front of Ashley. I should've asked Enrique if you were.

No, no, it's fine, Ashley said. I like meat.

When my mom headed back to the kitchen, Enrique's shoulder dipped, his arm reaching under the table. Ashley jumped in her seat and slapped Enrique on the shoulder, playfully. Behave, she whispered.

My mom served Enrique and then me before

finally sitting down with her own bowl. If you don't like the broccoli, you can just take them out, my mom said. I won't be hurt.

I like anything that's green, really.

My mom eyed Ashley's hair once more and smiled.

Ashley spooned a small stalk of broccoli out and lifted it to her mouth.

So how did you two meet anyway? my mom wanted to know.

Biology class, Enrique said. I sat behind her and copied all her answers. That's why I didn't do so well in that class.

Ashley slapped Enrique again. Playfully again.

Do you know any nice girls for my Marcus? my mom asked.

I almost choked on my stew. Stop, I said.

It would be nice, my mom continued. Then the four of you could all go out together. I think you spend too much time in your bedroom, Marcus. Always drawing or listening to music. I don't know how you got to be so passive.

I felt my cheeks fill with blood, my embarrassment glowing like neon.

Beth doesn't have a boyfriend, Ashley said, her voice optimistic. You know her, Marcus, right?

Who's Beth? my mom said brightly.

She's a girl who isn't my type, I said.

Well, then, what's your type?

Next subject.

Don't you want to meet someone?

Look, I said, annoyed. When are *you* going to start dating again? I asked. I wiped my mouth and looked straight at her.

Oh, don't be silly.

I don't think Mr. Cormac is married, Enrique said.

Yep, he's single, I said.

Ashley shook her head and placed her hand on top of Mom's. He has a potbelly and a comb-over and crooked teeth, she said.

They're not *that* crooked, I said.

Ashley laughed. He's not right for you, Mrs. Mendoza. Don't listen to your boys.

Oh, Enrique, he sounds terrible.

Yeah, well, beggars can't be choosers, I said. I picked up the saltshaker and shook some grains over the beef stew. It's not as flavorful as the last time you made it, I said.

My mom frowned. I'm not begging, she said. I'm happy where I'm at right now.

Ditto, I said, which wasn't true. I was jealous as hell that my brother—my *younger* brother—had a girl-friend over for dinner, someone as cute as Ashley, a girl my mother was warming up to. It didn't seem fair. I was the one who noticed her first. If I wasn't so damn shy, things could've turned out differently. Ashley could've been slapping me playfully on the shoulder instead of Enrique. And Enrique could've been the one who felt inadequate instead of me.

I leaned in and spooned stew into my mouth, the broth seasoned with diced onions and parsley. I felt Ashley's foot nudge mine before she pulled it quickly away.

Sorry, she said. I kicked your foot.

As if that's all she did to me.

It was the last week of July when exterminators came to cover up the house behind our house with a striped red and white tarp that turned it into a circus tent. Earlier that week, I heard a woman shout, *You're a beast!* followed by the sound of glass breaking. It was as if we were one big house: Our neighbors lived in the north wing and we lived in the south wing, the now much quieter wing. I imagined the poison spreading inside their darkened bedrooms, the living room and garage. I imagined a spider crawling up a wall and falling to the ground, curling up into a little black fist.

My mom was in the backyard, digging weeds out from the rectangle of grass by the swimming pool. She used a trowel and wore gardening gloves and dumped the weeds into a cardboard box.

Ashley's sweet, she said. Don't you think?

Yeah, she's cool, I said. I was sitting on a low brick wall, drawing my mom, hunched and digging into the world.

I didn't care too much for her hair.

I could tell. You kept looking at it.

Why do kids do that?

To be different.

But *green?* she said, yanking another weed out and dumping it into the box.

I'm going to dye my hair one of these days, I said.

You want to look like a clown, go ahead.

Hey, Mom, I said. She looked over at me and I pointed to our neighbor's house. At least we won't have to hear them for a while, I said.

She pushed the trowel into the grass. I know, she said. It reminds me of the house that I grew up in.

It reminds me of the house that *I* grew up in.

Oh, Marcus, it was never that bad.

Are you kidding? I put down my pencil and looked at my mother. There was a smudge of dirt on her forehead.

Your father and I never screamed at each other like that, she said. Maybe a few times, but not like *that*. She waved the trowel toward our neighbor's house, the tarp billowing like the sail of a ship.

I was talking about Enrique and Dad, not you and him, I said. Besides, I think you were in denial a little about what he was doing to Enrique.

I was shading the ground where she crouched over the grass, the pencil scratching the page, but when I glanced up I saw that my mom was now on her knees, sitting back on the heels of her shoes. I couldn't tell if she was hurt or angry or both. It was the first time we'd ever talked about this.

You don't think that I tried to talk to your father, that I tried to make him understand what Enrique was going through?

I hope you did.

Marcus, I tried. I *really* tried.

Well, it wasn't enough.

My mom stood and picked up the cardboard box and walked to the trash cans by the side of the house, dumping the weeds into one that was open and haloed in flies. Are you coming inside? she asked, still angry, her voice hammered flat.

After I finish this, I said, tapping the drawing with the end of my pencil. I'll just be a second.

I know you're still angry, she said.

I'm not.

I mean at your father.

Oh, I said.

I looked at our neighbor's house, the small waves that rolled across the tarp whenever the wind bothered it, and remembered again the sound of glass breaking. The next morning I saw the damage on one of their bedroom windows. A giant hole with teeth. An opening for any winged thing to fly through.

I thought about the day my dad brought my mom ten red tulips on their ten-year anniversary. I thought about this other side of my dad, the side whose eyes welled up when he hugged my uncle at the airport. The side that took me out for ice cream when my soccer team lost the finals. And the side that would scoop up Enrique from the couch whenever he fell asleep watching TV, carry him to bed gently so as not to disturb whatever dream he was having.

It was a Saturday, the sky overcast and the grass in our backyard still damp from the previous day's rain. Enrique and I were kicking a soccer ball back and forth. I was ten, he was nine. The ball went into the flower beds and Enrique went in, careful not to flatten any of my mom's daffodils or daisies. He high-stepped over the flowers and his shoes sunk into the soil and when my mom called us in for lunch, we sprinted inside the house.

Enrique, my dad shrieked from his sofa chair. My body flinched. I turned and saw the muddy tracks on the pale yellow carpet, the brown footprints that led to where Enrique stood. *Oh shit*, he said, chuckling. *Did I do that?* My dad pitched forward and swung and his hand clapped loudly against Enrique's face. He fell, stunned. He held his cheek with a small hand and cried and his face turned scarlet. *You think that's funny?* my dad said, pointing at the tracks.

I should've done something then as my dad kept yelling, his fury a black wind blowing through the living room, full of electricity. I should've said it was my fault, that I was the one who told Enrique to go into the flower beds and retrieve the ball. I should've done something, anything but cower in the corner and press my hands against my ears, which is exactly what I did. My dad lifted his hand again, swung again. I shook until I peed on myself, my jeans going dark down my pant leg, and I remember thinking, *Now he will beat me.*

Not once did my dad turn his rage on me. It happened to Enrique too often to have to do with timing, and it wasn't that I was lucky, either. It had something to do with what was inside of me. Or, rather, what was *not* inside of me. Maybe he recognized in Enrique what was his, not only the shape of his eyes and the slope of his nose, but his sharp tongue.

Once, when a glass of orange juice slipped from my hand in the kitchen, I quickly dropped to my knees on the tile. I was already picking up the shards and crying when he found me. *That's okay, Mijo*, he said. *Don't cry, Mijo.* He joined me on the floor and, in a calm voice he rarely used with Enrique, he demonstrated how I should pick up only the big pieces, being careful not to cut myself, then used a wet paper towel to mop up the tiny shards we couldn't see.

I was ashamed for never defending Enrique, but I was also relieved my dad never hit me. I told myself that Enrique got hit because he talked back, but I knew it was more than that. My dad didn't beat me because he knew I was weak, because he knew I punished myself enough.

Until I turned thirteen, Enrique and I shared a room. We had a bunk bed—I had the bottom bunk and he had the top. On a day when Enrique was beaten, I felt him thinking hard above me. He would turn over and over and the bedsprings would squeak.

You can't sleep? I'd ask.

Nuh-uh, he'd say.

One time, when neither of us could sleep, I asked him if he could live anywhere on earth, where would it be.

Antarctica, he said.

Antarctica?

They have lots of penguins.

But it's so cold, I explained. No one lives there, Enrique.

I know, he said. I'd like that.

I turned over and looked around our bedroom, the black outlines of the chair and desk, the deep navy blue of the window. In the corner, our Casper the Friendly Ghost night-light glowed a pale green.

Good night, I said.

What's good about it? he said.

5

WHEN MY DAD LEFT, he drove away in his inky black Corvette, a sleek thing with tan leather seats and gills above the front tires. We were left with a Chevrolet Caprice station wagon. The top half was light blue, the bottom half a blond wood grain. It was sky and desert on wheels. The steering wheel felt like a hula hoop in my hands. I had no chance of getting laid in a car like that. Absolutely none. Not that my introverted self was helping things.

I pulled up to the curb under the shade of an oak tree. I looked around and checked my mirrors, making sure no one was watching me in this hideous thing I drove. The neighborhood was empty except for an old man watering his lawn three houses down.

I hurried up the walkway and rang Oliver's door-bell. Their one-story house had a backboard nailed above the garage, the rim bent so far down it was almost perpendicular to the driveway. From the street it looked like a red zero.

Britt answered the door. He was already stoned, his hair full of cowlicks. The barrel of his starter pistol was shoved down the front of his jeans with the black handle resting against his white T-shirt. What up, Nine? he said.

I pointed at the gun. Do you know how fuckin' stu-pid that looks?

Britt shrugged.

Is that Nub? Oliver yelled out, his voice deep inside the house.

He's *all* messed up, Britt said, thumbing over his shoulder.

I'm sure he is, I said, and stepped inside.

Oliver's house smelled like old leather and Pine-Sol. Two brown couches faced each other in the liv-ing room. There was a wooden coffee table between them littered with empty soda cans, crumpled napkins, and an open pizza box with one lone slice inside. Candles stood on opposite ends of the mantel above the fireplace, a row of framed photographs in between: Oliver at three, at six, at ten. Oliver dressed for Halloween and Oliver in a Little League baseball uniform. Oliver fishing with his father. Mrs. Thompson holding a piece of wedding cake for Mr. Thompson, his mouth wide open and ready to bite.

Oliver was crouched by the stereo. Check this out, he said, and pushed the PLAY button. The room exploded with drums and bass, a guitar riff drenched in feedback.

That sounds good, I said. Who's that?

Trigger Cut, Oliver said. They're local.

I like it.

I knew you would. I'll burn you a copy.

You guys heard about Darren, right? Britt asked.

What about him? Oliver said.

He moved to Alaska.

Shut up.

I'm serious.

What the hell for?

To live with his mom, Britt said. Pops wasn't too happy about him getting that room at the

Travelodge. It was the last straw, I guess.

I pictured Darren in the coldest region of Alaska, wearing a heavy jacket and ski cap, bits of ice crusted in his brows and eyelashes. I pictured him lifting a frozen beer bottle to his lips, then turning it upside down and smacking the bottom as if it were a bottle of ketchup.

When's your mom coming back? I asked.

In a couple hours. If you want to smoke a bowl, do it now, he said. And do it outside. Mom's got a nose like a bloodhound.

Twenty minutes later and the three of us were sitting at the dinner table, bent over a half-finished puzzle. At the top of the box it said *The Kiss by Gustav Klimt*. Some guy in a checkered gold robe was kissing some girl on her cheek, a redhead kneeling on a cliff, her bare feet hanging over the edge. The whole thing shimmered like the scales of a fish. I looked at the puzzle and picked up a piece and turned it inches from my face. Wow, I whispered.

I know, Britt said.

I can't believe you guys did half of this already.

My mom did, Oliver said. We haven't done shit.

My face was numb. Britt said he'd gotten some potent weed from Hawaii, *gourmet marijuana,* he'd called it, but now I wondered if it was laced. It felt like someone shot me point-blank with novocaine. When I rubbed my hand over my face, my nose and cheeks felt rubbery. Hey, guys, I said. Do this.

Do what? Britt asked.

This, I said, and rubbed my hand over my face again. It feels strange.

Oliver slid his hand over his face. You're right, he said.

Britt was next, sliding from his forehead all the way down to his chin. Oh man, he said. My head is made of Nerf.

We all started laughing uncontrollably.

Excuse me, gentlemen, I said, but it's time for me to drain the main vein.

In the bathroom I held on to the towel rack above the toilet and aimed, still chuckling. I sprayed the floor a little and when I finished I grabbed some toilet paper and kneeled to wipe the tile. Something small rattled across the floor. It was a piece of plastic from a disposable razor, the transparent strip that covered the blade. Oliver's face was as smooth as mine, so I knew it must've been his father's. I wondered if he'd shaved on the day he walked down to the basement and looped the extension cord over the I-beam, or if he'd looked at his face in the mirror that morning, dragged his fingers across the bristles, and left the razor where it was, knowing what he planned to do later. I picked up the strip of plastic, wrapped it in toilet paper, and tossed it into the wastebasket.

When I stepped out of the bathroom I could hear Britt and Oliver still laughing. I looked down the hallway, the half-open door of the master bedroom, and suddenly I was floating there. Whatever hang-ups I had about snooping in my best friend's mother's bedroom a five-leafed plant from Hawaii put them to rest.

The bed was king-size, the flower-printed bedcover sunk slightly over two faint dimples on the mattress where Mr. and Mrs. Thompson slept together for two decades. On top of the dresser was a hairbrush, a jewelry box, more framed photographs. There were quite a few of Mr. and Mrs. Thompson together, in different vacation spots. One looked like Europe, one looked like Hong Kong. In another they stood on a beach with sunlight on their faces, the photographer's purple shadow stretched on the sand. I wondered who snapped the picture, if it was a stranger or someone they knew. There was a white sailboat in the background and the sails were full of wind, its bow pointed right at Mr. Thompson's neck. Mrs. Thompson wore a red two-piece bathing suit, her hair all messed up from the breeze. She had sexy legs, a flat stomach and narrow waist. I wanted something that belonged to her, something close to her skin. I thought about her panties and as soon as I did I started opening drawers, beginning with the top left. Magazines, a date book, pens and pencils, loose change. Three rows of empty drawers and two rows of stacked sweaters. A drawer with nothing but balled-up socks. Finally, I found her underwear drawer.

Yo, *Digit*, Oliver shouted. *Did you fall in?*

Stop polishing your sword, Britt yelled.

I grabbed a neglected pair bunched up in the back of the drawer, lacy and black, and shoved them down the front of my jeans. I closed the drawer and checked myself in the mirror above the dresser and hurried out, remembering to keep the bedroom door like it was, half closed.

In the hallway I stood a moment watching Oliver. He curled his fingers around imaginary drumsticks and smacked the air around him and I thought: *I'm a boy without a father, watching a boy without a father banging on invisible drums.*

What took you so long? Oliver asked when I sat back down at the table.

Britt moved his fist up and down, making that mosquito sound with his mouth.

I pissed on the floor and had to clean it up, I said.

You mean you *jizzed* on the floor, Britt said.

At least I have meat to beat, I said. How do you stroke your cashew, like this? I rubbed my thumb and forefinger together in the air.

Oliver laughed. Britt laughed harder, doubling over. I was confused until I realized he was pointing at my stub. *Oh shit, oh shit*, he said, teary-eyed. Look at his *nub*, he said.

Fuck you, I said.

Oliver's laughter trailed off. He looked down at the puzzle. Okay, shut up, Bongoloid, he said. Let's try to find at least one that fits.

We studied the puzzle again, all those freckled gold pieces, our heads bowed over the table. We didn't move. From the outside it might've looked like we were saying grace.

An hour later we had destroyed a bag of potato chips and pretzels and washed it down with glass after glass of orange juice. We watched music videos and *Celebrity Deathmatch* and eventually my head stopped feeling synthetic.

Mom's here, Oliver said when we heard the garage door growl open. Hide your toy gun, Stonehenge.

It's not a toy.

Whatever, just hide it.

Britt lifted the front of his shirt and stretched it over the handle of the starter pistol.

Mrs. Thompson walked in holding her purse. She'd been at the salon and her hair now looked inflated and shiny. Well, guys, what do you think? she asked. She turned around slowly to show us every angle.

Why is it so fluffy? Oliver asked.

It is kind of big, Britt added, looking mildly comatose on the couch.

Mrs. Thompson had walked in the house glowing,

but now her face slouched.

I think it looks good, I said, immediately embarrassed. I could feel Oliver's eyes on me.

Why, thank you, Marcus, she said. So what have you guys been up to?

We were working on the puzzle, Oliver said.

Mrs. Thompson walked over to the dinner table. It doesn't look like you made any progress.

We found a few, I said.

Yeah, Oliver said. We did.

Uh-huh, Britt mumbled.

Mrs. Thompson gave Oliver an accusatory look before heading to her bedroom.

What? Oliver shouted.

Don't play innocent with me, she shouted back.

It was time for us to leave. Oliver had to get ready for his new job bussing tables and delivering pizza for Antonio's Pizzeria. Britt had to mow the lawn before his father came home from work. As for myself, I had nothing to do and nowhere to be.

While Oliver was in his room putting on his uniform (a red baseball cap and shirt with Antonio's logo—a mustached man riding a bicycle with pizza pies for tires), Mrs. Thompson walked me to the front door.

I really dig your hair, I said again.

I have to get used to it, she said, patting the side of it with her hand.

I almost forgot I had her panties shoved down the front of my jeans. And now I was talking to her, complimenting her new hairdo with her lacy underwear pressed against my crotch. I felt ashamed and embarrassed even though she had no idea what I was hiding. I said good-bye and headed down the walkway. When I reached the piece-of-shit-mobile I looked back, hoping Mrs. Thompson was checking me out, but the front door was already closed.

I had nowhere else to go but back home, up to my clothes-strewn and postered bedroom. With my door locked, I played one of Oliver's mix CDs on my portable stereo. The Wrens, the Black Keys, Deerhoof, Modest Mouse—it was one fierce song after another. I pulled out Mrs. Thompson's black panties, my head still a little woozy from the weed. Her panties were sheer, the edges ridged with lace. There were flowers embroidered on the meshed fabric and each stem curled into five petals. It was like her funeral veil, those tiny dark roses that floated over her ruined face. I lifted the panties to my nose and breathed in.

All I could smell was dust.

We used to play this game at the Cerritos Shopping Center. It wasn't a game, really—no points were added, no score was kept. We didn't have any money, just enough for a pack of bubble gum, which is all we needed. One of us chewed a piece of gum, usually Britt, and afterward he'd push the wad into the spout of one of the drinking fountains. Then we'd sit at a nearby bench and wait, the mall echoing with the voices of shoppers, a constant droning.

We would wait and wait, anxious for a laugh at someone else's expense, because we were loaded, because the world didn't care about us and vice versa.

Soon enough someone was heading straight toward the fountain, oblivious.

I remembered a middle-aged man in specs leaning in, how the water shot out and how his head snapped back, the white handkerchief he removed from his back pocket to wipe the lenses.

I remembered a young woman full of shopping bags, the water spraying her chin, her blouse, how she cursed at us when she saw us laughing on the bench, holding our stomachs.

And the little Asian girl in pigtails, on tiptoes to reach the arc of water, only to be hit with a stream directly in the eye. The way she bawled, the way her mother consoled her. *Oh, honey*, she said, rubbing the back of her head. *It's only water, sweetie.*

I was sitting on the bench, alone now, remembering all of this, when I saw Ashley walk into the Hallmark store across the way. I didn't see her face, actually, but I recognized the green shade of her hair, the plaid pattern of her skirt. I imagined she was smiling and that she was at the Hallmark store to pick out a card for Enrique. It was early August and his birthday was only a week away. You lucky bastard, I thought. You lucky depressive fuck.

I decided to take out the Valium Oliver had given me earlier that day. At the very fountain we once sabotaged I swallowed the white pill and when I turned around a boy with Down syndrome was sitting on the far end of the bench. He had a bowl cut and a Mickey

Mouse T-shirt tucked into his slacks. I looked around, trying to find his parents.

Hello, he said.

I sat beside him. What's up, little man? I said.

He shrugged his shoulders. He looked down at his shoes and swung them lazily, back and forth over the polished floor.

Where're your mom and dad? I asked.

My mom's buying cookies, he said, pointing at the bakery. You want one?

No, thanks.

Okay, he said. He swung his shoes faster now, back and forth, back and forth, like a windup toy. I thought that if Enrique were here, he'd make fun of him. He could be heartless that way.

The boy tapped the back of my hand. What happened to your finger? he asked.

I had an accident.

Did it hurt?

I passed out, so I didn't feel anything.

What's passed out?

I blacked out, I said.

The boy's mouth was half open and his pink tongue

rested on his bottom lip. His almond-shaped eyes were brown and blank as stones. He didn't know what the hell I was saying.

I fell asleep, I finally said. And then I woke up in the hospital.

The boy smiled, his round face lighting up. I could tell he liked the idea of transportation by sleeping, that you could close your eyes in one part of the world and wake up in another.

I didn't know what else to tell him. I just wanted the Valium to kick in.

I had an accident, too, he said, breaking the silence. He bent his arm and lifted it up. There was a SpongeBob Band-Aid on his elbow, a spot of dried blood the color of rust.

What happened? I asked.

I was running and I tripped and I fell—like this, he said, stretching his arms out.

Ouch, I said. You have to be careful.

I didn't fall asleep, he said.

No, that only happens when it *really* hurts.

So it really hurt when you lost your finger? he said, looking at my hand.

I guess it did.

And then you fell asleep?

Yeah, then I fell asleep, I said, finally feeling the Valium.

Enrique and I were at the grocery store when I literally bumped into Beth Guzman, Ashley's friend. Our shopping carts crashed as I turned down the cereal aisle.

I hope you don't drive the same way, Beth said, smiling.

Sorry about that, I said.

What have you been up to? She took a strand of hair and pulled it behind her ear. I didn't know what to say. My tongue was pretzeled inside my mouth. Beth looked at Enrique, who was trying to decide between Wheaties and Raisin Bran. Is that your little brother? she asked.

Yep, I said.

Enrique yanked the shopping cart from my grasp and dropped the Raisin Bran inside.

Ashley really likes you, Beth said.

I really like me, too. Enrique smirked and left us alone.

What a brat, Beth said.

At least you don't have to live with him.

I haven't seen you since the Travelodge.

That was a crazy party, I said, remembering how Beth was topless, how she straddled some guy I didn't know with fingers that crawled up her naked back, spiderlike. I'm never doing acid again, I added.

My cousin used to date this guy who did it once and he had flashbacks all the time. Like a giant black hole would open up in the sky and he'd start to freak out.

Great.

You'll probably be fine, she said, pulling another strand of hair behind her ear.

My palms dampened.

On the intercom, a price check was called for the fried pork rinds.

We should grab coffee sometime, Beth said.

Yes, definitely.

Beth searched inside her purse and pulled out a pen and scribbled her number on the back of a movie ticket stub. Enrique rolled back with the shopping cart. He took the Raisin Bran out and placed it back on the shelf and reached for the Wheaties.

Nights are best to get a hold of me, she said. Anytime after six.

Great, I said, sliding her number into my back pocket.

When Beth was out of earshot, I punched Enrique on the arm. What the hell? I said.

What?

You barely even acknowledged her. That's Ashley's friend.

I know. She's a slut.

No, she's not.

Ashley's told me stories.

Some friend, I said. Maybe she's also telling Beth stories about you.

Yeah, right.

How well do you know her?

Well enough to know that she wouldn't talk shit behind my back.

I made a humph sound.

Man, fuck you, Enrique said.

We reached the only open checkout line at the same time as an old man. He wore a flannel shirt and a trucker hat and smelled of stale tobacco. His shopping cart was completely full. At the top of the heap was a loaf of wheat bread, a box of tissues, and a blue bottle of Windex. Our cart only had four items.

Sir, Enrique said. Can we go ahead of you?

The old man began to place his items on the conveyer belt.

Hello? You deaf? Enrique said. Which he was—a cream-colored hearing aid was fitted into his left ear. I said are you *deaf*?

He looked at Enrique, and my brother got right up in the old man's face. I grabbed Enrique's arm at the elbow. Stop, I said. The old man turned away from us and continued placing his items on the conveyer belt. The pimply girl at the register looked at Enrique, her eyes full of worry. I could tell she was wondering if she needed to call security.

After she rang up the old man and he walked away, I told her I was sorry. She just smacked her bubblegum and scanned our items without saying a word.

Enrique was already in the parking lot by the time I pushed the cart outside. He was walking fast and suddenly broke into a jog. I was confused—we had parked in the opposite direction. Then I saw the elderly man, placing a bag of groceries into the trunk of his car, and

Enrique heading right toward him. I shouted his name. Twice, three times. Still, Enrique raised his hand and slapped the hat off the old man's head, sending it tumbling end over end onto the pavement.

Once we were back inside the car, Enrique rolled down the window and hocked a loogie into the night.

That was messed up, I said.

He shot a look at me, his face rigid and his eyes wild with rage. It was as if Dad had returned and was now sitting in the passenger seat, and this time his fists would come spiraling my way.

When he reached for the radio, I flinched. Enrique looked at me. Don't be such a pussy, he said.

I was embarrassed, but I was more angry that Enrique didn't realize he was becoming the person he despised so much, that there were other ways to act.

We drove home in silence. I glanced at my brother, who was looking at the trees rushing past the passenger-side window. His head was still as if he was deep in thought. Maybe he realized it then—as long as he didn't raise a fist or scream out in anger, our dad was truly out of our lives.

6

IT WAS EARLY AUGUST and hot as a furnace. Every breeze felt like a large blow-dryer was pointed right at me. I stayed inside most of the day, downloading music and watching TV.

My mom walked in with a serious look on her face. I hit MUTE on the remote.

Did Grandma die? I said.

No.

What happened then?

It's your father, she said. He wants to come back.

I felt the blood leave my face, my heart thumping under my shirt. Please tell me you're joking, I said.

She looked out my bedroom window.

Did you talk to him or something? I asked.

We've been talking, she said. Yes.

For how long?

For the last couple of months. He's been sending me money.

What the hell for? I was yelling. I was shocked.

Marcus, we can't afford to live in this house, she said. I don't get that much waitressing at the Palace. Without your father's checks, we would be living in a motel.

Jesus, I said. Why didn't you tell me?

I'm telling you now.

I mean before.

Mijo, I wasn't sure how to tell you.

What about Enrique? Have you told Enrique? He's going to flip out.

I'm going to tell him this afternoon, she said.

My mom sat on the edge of my bed and looked out my bedroom window again. There was nothing to see but our street and the Phillipses' yard and stucco house. They had a red and white BEWARE OF DOG sign on their gate even though their dog died years ago. I don't know what to do, my mom finally said.

My heart was still going crazy under my shirt. Where is he? I asked.

In Monterey, she said. He's doing construction work again, building houses.

I don't believe this, I said, shaking my head.

He wants to see both of you, she said. He wants to apologize.

Oh, he does now, does he?

Yes, he does.

I don't believe this, I said again. I picked up my sketchbook and pencil and began doodling spirals down the page, black smoke coiling out of nowhere.

He wants to talk to you.

No, I said.

I don't think it would hurt you to talk to him.

I said no.

My mom stood up and sighed. Just think about it, okay? she said.

As if I could think about anything else.

For hours I thought about it. In my bedroom with music, with the blinds closed, I thought about it. After my mom told Enrique we both thought about it in our separate rooms.

Our dad. Our goddamn dad.

In the hallway, Enrique and I bumped into each other. He looked distraught, his hair wild as if he'd slept on it. This fuckin' sucks, he said.

No kidding, I said.

I told Mom I'd run away if he ever came back.

I don't blame you.

Where the hell's Monterey, anyway? Enrique wanted to know.

In California. Up north somewhere, I think.

Is it close?

I'm not sure.

Let's find out.

Enrique followed me into my bedroom and I opened up my Web browser. A few mouse clicks later and a map of central California came up. There, I said, pointing at the yellow star on the map. It's pretty close to San Francisco.

Sonofabitch, Enrique muttered. His face was rigid, the muscle along his jaw line flexed.

I was pissed too, and as I had at Mr. Thompson's funeral, I imagined killing my dad. With a hammer, a bat. With my own two fists.

Enrique stared at the monitor and bit on his thumbnail. He turned to me. I've got an idea, he said.

What? I said.

Let's go to Monterey.

Are you serious?

Dead serious, he said.

And do what?

Enrique smiled wickedly.

A half hour later we were all talked out. Enrique's eyes were wide, excited. The plan was reckless, yes, but there was something appealing about it. Maybe a part of me was also becoming like my dad.

Later on that evening I casually asked my mom for his address. She was in the kitchen, chopping carrots into fat orange tokens on a cutting board. I want to send him a card or something before I talk to him, I said.

My mom put the knife down and wiped her hands on a dish towel. Why the sudden change? she said, looking right at me.

I just, you know, I said, stammering.

My mom studied my face. You just what?

I just would rather send him a card first, that's all.

There's a few things I have to get off my chest, I said. I don't think I could say it to him over the phone.

Okay, Mijo, she said. She brushed the back of my head with her fingers.

Minutes later she returned with his address written on a piece of paper and folded in half. If you want, I could help you pick out a nice card.

No, thanks, I said. I can do it myself.

She lifted the knife again. I'm proud of you, she said, chopping. I'm really proud of you.

Holy shit, Oliver said.

We were standing in front of the abandoned house where the drug addict was shacked up with his cat. Half of the house was eaten away by a fire and the other half was charred black. We could see the sky through the ribs of the roof.

Damn, I said. What the hell happened?

There was a fire.

Duh. I mean I wonder how it started.

The junkie, Oliver said. That's how.

You think he died?

Probably.

There was yellow CAUTION tape around the front yard, turning and twisting in the wind. The fire was days old, but the scent of its burning was still in the air. The chimney stood naked in a pile of debris like a brick monolith.

I thought of the fire alarm in my own house, how one night it chirped incessantly in the middle of the night and woke everyone up. Enrique and I stood in our pajamas, rubbing our eyes as we watched our dad pull the fire alarm from the ceiling. He opened the back side and yanked out the battery. Go back to bed, he told us. But I couldn't. Nothing would warn us now if a fire started somewhere in the house, swallowing the curtains, the walls, the furniture, and finally us.

So tomorrow, Oliver said.

Yes, tomorrow, I said.

We should leave early so we don't hit any traffic.

Good idea.

Hey, we have to take my dad's car.

How come?

The horn, he said. My mom doesn't want me to drive that far without a horn.

That sucks.

No kidding.

Just as we were about to pull away from the curb I saw the junkie's cat coming out of the bushes. She looked mangier than ever and was meowing like crazy. I opened the passenger door and the cat hopped in. She wouldn't stop meowing.

Shut that thing *off*, Oliver said as we drove.

Dude, she's hungry.

We pulled into the drive-through at Taco Bell and ordered a burrito for the cat. When I held it up to her mouth, she sniffed the warm tortilla a few times before she took a bite. Then she was devouring it, ground beef and little strips of lettuce falling onto my lap. By the time we got to Britt's house the burrito was gone. She slid her tongue over her black lips and blinked in the sun. We named her Catface.

'Sup, bitches? Britt said. He was pushing a lawn mower out of the garage and down the driveway.

'Sup, Bongoloid, I yelled from inside the car. You got the you-know-what?

Yeah, hold on a sec.

Britt left the mower by the grass and trotted back into the garage. Catface sat up on my lap and I rubbed the back of her head and she purred, a little motor revving inside her throat.

She probably has rabies, Oliver said.

Cats don't get rabies.

Mangy cats do.

Don't make me sic her on you.

She's got rabies, man. I can tell.

Catface, sic Oliver, I said. *Sic 'im!*

Britt walked up to the truck and pointed the gun at my head. You talkin' shit, Freak Show?

You crazy sonofabitch, I yelled.

Calm down, Nub. It's not loaded.

I don't care, I said, and pulled the gun from his hand, irritated.

Don't lose it, man.

Can I take this thing off? I said, fingering the red plastic ring at the end of the barrel.

Go ahead.

I dug my fingernail under and peeled off the plastic ring and handed it to Britt. I slipped out the gun's cylinder and made sure all the chambers were empty.

You sure you don't want to come with us? Oliver asked.

I can't, Britt said. I've got to help my dad paint the garage this weekend. Whose cat is that?

Mine, I said.

So you finally got pussy.

I aimed the starter pistol at Britt and squeezed the trigger. It clicked loudly like a snapped pencil.

I went to the market later that night, this time with a short list. Just eggs and milk and tinfoil. I was opening up a carton of eggs, making sure none of them were busted, when Mrs. Thompson came up to me rolling an empty cart.

You're going to think I'm following you, she said.

I laughed. How are you doing, Mrs. Thompson?

Gloria, she corrected me.

That's right, I'm sorry.

That's okay.

How are you doing, Gloria?

I'm getting by, she said. It's still hard, you know? She leaned on her empty cart.

I'm sure it is, I said. I can't even imagine, I added. I didn't know what else to tell her. There should be a book, some manual out there for situations like this:

How to Talk to a Widow Without Sounding Like a Dipshit.

So Oliver told me the two of you are driving to Las Vegas, she said.

We sure are, I said, which was a lie. Oliver said he'd drive us to Monterey if we could go to San Francisco afterward to try to score some drugs from his uncle. We told our parents that we were going to Las Vegas to see Cirque du Soleil.

When are you guys leaving?

Tomorrow morning.

You keep a close eye on my Oliver, okay?

I always do, I said. Another lie. I was racking them up.

I need some eggs too, she said, reaching for a carton. She opened the lid and the next thing I knew she was crying. With one hand she covered her eyes while the other still held on to the open carton of eggs. I took the carton away from her and placed it back on the shelf.

You'll be okay, I said, even though I had no idea if she would.

I'm sorry, I'm sorry, she said, her voice cracking. I

miss him. I still love him.

I know, I said. And then I said something completely stupid: He still loves you, too. Which was a truckload of crap, really. Mr. Thompson was underground in a casket with a heart pickled in embalming fluid. He wasn't ever going to be able to love Mrs. Thompson again.

I gave her a hug and remembered I had her lacy underwear stashed in the back of my closet. Standing there, my arms around her, hers around mine, I suddenly wanted to be completely loaded. I wanted my head numb and the world distorted around me. Everything was too vivid—the chicken breasts wrapped in plastic, the shopping carts that rattled behind me, the humming freezer, the child singing in the next aisle.

She continued sobbing.

It's okay, I said. I looked at the shelf of eggs over her shoulder and thought about their brittle shells.

7

OUR DAD'S RAGE FOLLOWED us after he left. It trailed behind our footsteps from room to room, invisible. Sometimes we could see it, like the holes Enrique made in his bedroom, or the sheets of paper I scribbled on violently with a pencil held in my fist. Now we were taking our rage straight back to its source.

Oliver pulled up to my house in his dead father's car, a gunmetal blue Buick. It had a bumper sticker that announced the owner of the vehicle cared about the environment despite the dark plume of smoke the muffler coughed out whenever we accelerated after a stop. We dubbed the car "the Picklewagon."

I didn't know Ashley was coming along until she

showed up that morning with her backpack and green hair rubber-banded into a ponytail. Enrique was holding Catface, scratching her throat. I pulled him to the side. Does she know what we're doing? I whispered.

He shook his head no.

Good, I said.

Ashley snuck up on Enrique and pinched his ass. What're you two whispering about? she wanted to know.

Personal stuff, I said.

Oliver slapped the roof of the car. Come on, he said. Let's go.

We climbed into the car and headed down South Street and onto the 605. In the backseat, Enrique was tickling Ashley, who giggled and tried to tickle him back. He said he was tickle-proof and sat still to prove it. Ashley's fingers went over his stomach as if she were playing a piano. Nothing.

See? Enrique said. I was born without a funny bone.

Ashley leaned close to Enrique's ear and whispered a few words and he grinned. That's true, my brother said. That's so very true.

Enough already, you two, Oliver said from behind the wheel, his eyes on the rearview mirror. You're going to make me blow chunks.

Ditto, I said.

I twisted the radio dial from the passenger seat, every station fizzed with static. I turned the knob forward and back, forward and back, determined to find a song, any song. I found a Marvin Gaye tune before a wave of static crashed over his voice.

Open the glove box, Oliver said. Maybe there's some CDs.

I clicked open the glove compartment and rummaged through its contents. There was a road map and a pink takeout menu from a Chinese restaurant. There was the little white kite of a dead moth. There was an envelope from Kodak plump with photographs and I flipped through them casually as if they belonged to me. There were pictures of a narrow house wedged between two more narrow houses. A red front door and tiny foyer. A living room with a shag rug and a glass coffee table, a black leather couch. A bedroom with too many pillows piled against the headboard. A photo of a woman taken outdoors, surrounded by foliage.

She was in her midforties, blond curls with the wind caught in them, big eyes and a big smile.

I held the picture up for Oliver. Who's this? I asked.

Oliver glanced over at the photograph. I don't know, he said.

Then another photograph of the same woman, this time sitting beside Mr. Thompson at a restaurant. I held this up to Oliver.

Oh, yeah, he said, pausing. That's my aunt. I didn't recognize her.

Ashley coughed. The car grew quiet.

Don't be so damn nosy, Oliver said. I thought you were looking for CDs.

Yeah, man, Enrique chimed in from the backseat.

Ashley slapped Enrique on the arm.

What? he said.

Oliver kept his eyes on the road and said nothing. No one knew why his father killed himself, but I felt as though the answer, at least part of it, was in my hands, bracketed on a 3x5 glossy. I slipped the photos back inside the envelope and shoved them in the glove compartment.

We hit some traffic when we reached the 5 freeway

heading north. Catface jumped onto my lap and pushed her head under my hand so I would run my fingers down her back, which I did. She squinted and purred.

Ashley leaned in, her head between the headrests. Catface looks stoned, she said. Then added, She looks like Marcus did at the party.

I wasn't stoned, I said.

Whatever, you looked like that.

What party? Enrique wanted to know.

The hotel party a couple months ago, Oliver said. At the Travelodge.

Oh, *that*. I wasn't invited.

I invited you, I said.

No, you didn't.

Yes, I did, I said, pretending I was getting agitated. Truth is, I didn't invite him. He was moody as hell that day and I didn't want him around.

A silver sports car swerved in front of us a few feet from the bumper and Oliver pushed down on the horn.

Asshole, Enrique said from behind my headrest.

Just before Oliver picked us up that morning my mom told me to look after Enrique. He was in the bathroom, brushing his teeth and spitting into the sink.

Has he said anything to you? she asked.

What do you mean?

About your father?

Not really.

He's been more quiet than usual.

Ever since my mom told him that our dad wanted to talk to us and eventually come home, something inside Enrique recoiled. He moved around the house like a jaguar, his head low. I half expected him to punch another wall and make another hole. He'd sit in front of the television with his dumbbells and lift them to his chin, a vein bulging alongside his forearm like an earthworm.

Just keep an eye on him, my mom said.

I know.

Call me when you can.

I will.

Make sure he takes his medication.

Mom, I said. Stop worrying. If worrying were an Olympic sport, you'd get the gold medal.

I can't help it, she said.

We'll be back on Monday, okay?

Okay. Just watch your little brother.
Okay.

We hurtled up the interstate and there was nothing to look at on either side of the highway but flatlands. After we drove past some almond groves, it was miles and miles of dried brush. I let my eyes follow the telephone wires that slid up and down above the horizon. It was hypnotic—the ballet of wires, their rising and falling. For a handful of seconds it quieted my mind and I forgot what Enrique and I were scheming to do. It was his idea to drive to Monterey and confront our dad. It was his idea to put him in his place, to hear our dad explain himself before whipping out the pistol and making him feel the way he had always made Enrique feel.

I pulled the pistol out of my backpack and examined it closely. With the red plastic ring off, it looked like a regular gun. I wondered what he would do when it came time for Enrique to shove it in his face. And I wondered what Enrique would say, how he would handle all that power.

I looked over at my brother in the backseat. The

antidepressants always made him drowsy in the afternoon and his eyes were now closed, his head rested against the smudgy window of the Buick. Still, it amazed me that he was able to sleep—we were going eighty miles per hour toward a man who had tortured him for years. There was adrenaline in my heart as my mind spiraled and shuffled pictures of my dad, his rage, Enrique, his blood, the gun. There was no way I could possibly sleep.

Ashley scraped off her nail polish and dropped the flakes of maroon into the car's ashtray. When she saw me looking at her and not Enrique, she winked. I turned back to the road ahead that rolled under the car like a giant conveyer belt.

Sometimes I fantasized that Ashley was with me and not my brother, which I did then, post-wink. I imagined us doing it in a movie theater, on a Ferris wheel, a ski lift. I pictured her on top of me in the backseat of a convertible speeding toward a canyon, both of us coming at the same time in the air before we pull the ripcord on our parachutes and watch the convertible explode into a bouquet of flames on the canyon floor.

Enrique snored quietly, his mouth cracked open.

I want to make a little pit stop, if you don't mind, Oliver said.

Not at all, I said.

It would be good to stretch out my legs, Ashley added. She arched her back and twisted her body to the side. Her shirt rose above her skirt and I could see the butterfly tattoo inked there, perched on her hip-bone, the wings splayed and green.

The highway curved and Oliver took the next exit and made a left down another road and soon I could see the planes glittering on the horizon, lined up in a row like toys.

What's that? Ashley said.

It's an airplane graveyard, Oliver said. The world's largest, supposedly.

No shit, I said.

When we were close enough to see the logos on the tailfins—the dark blue arrow of Delta, Virgin Atlantic's scrawled handwriting, the abstract and smiling face of Alaska Airlines—Ashley fished out her digital camera from her backpack. What a trip, she said, and took a picture. There must be at least two hundred of them.

Look at the doors and windows, Oliver said. They're all taped over.

How come?

Probably to keep the dust out, I said.

What I want to know is how the pilots who flew these planes got back to wherever they came from. Ashley snapped another picture.

Good question.

Oliver pulled off to the side of the road. Let's check them out, he said.

What about him? Ashley motioned toward Enrique, who was still sleeping with his head against the window.

Screw him, I said.

I already did, Ashley said, smiling.

Oliver walked ahead and his boots kicked up beige clouds of dust. He hopped over the chain-link fence first, then me. Ashley climbed the fence last because she didn't want Oliver or me to peek under her skirt while she went over. Once we all made it over the fence we headed toward a 747. In the chrome of the fuselage we could see our reflections, distorted like a carnival mirror. Ashley reached up and slid her hand across the aircraft as if she were petting a whale. *Jesus*, she said to herself.

Oliver dug up a stone and tossed it at the plane's tailfin and it gonged like a church bell.

I never felt so puny as I felt while standing beside that massive plane, next to a girl I wanted but couldn't have, in a place that was no place at all. I reached up and pressed my palm against the airplane and felt the cold metal.

Can I ask you something? Ashley said.

Sounds serious.

Not really.

What is it?

Well, Ashley said. Your hand.

I took my hand away from the aircraft and held it before her, wiggling the stump. Let me guess, I said. You want to know what happened.

I already know. Your brother told me.

Oh.

I was wondering if you could still feel it.

What do you mean, like a phantom limb?

Yeah.

I lifted my hand and curled and uncurled my fingers.

Sometimes I feel like I can, I said. You know when there's a word on the tip of your tongue, and no matter how hard you think and concentrate, the word won't appear?

Yeah?

It sort of feels like that.

Ashley smiled. The stud in her nose shined in the bright sun. The wind played with her hair and it ribboned across her face. I wanted to kiss her. Another one of Oliver's rocks gonged against the 747.

Ashley pointed at the ground. *Lizard, lizard!* she cried out, all excited.

The lizard was small, about six inches long from head to tail. Its scaly skin was made of miniature octagons in different shades of gray. He lay very still on the ground with his reptilian head cocked in our direction. When Enrique and I were kids, I used to catch lizards in our backyard. I'd pull off their tail and we'd watch it move by itself, side to side like a windshield wiper. *Are you sure he'll grow another tail?* Enrique wanted to know.

Positive, I said.

It would be cool if people could do that too.

Later on that day I fetched a pair of rusty scissors from the garage. I looked inside the green bucket where I held the lizard captive and reached in. The lizard scrambled around, frantic, but still I managed to snip off one of its arms. I wanted to see if it would grow another one. I wanted to see if the severed arm would move all by itself the way its tail had, but it just lay there, useless. The next day I looked inside the bucket to see if the lizard had a new arm, but he wasn't moving. A fly crawled up his back.

A few weeks later I had the accident and lost my finger and I knew better than to hope that it might grow back.

I have to take a leak, Oliver said as we headed back to the Picklewagon, kicking up dust. He jogged a few yards out into a field while Ashley and I climbed in the car. Enrique was still zonked out in the backseat, his mouth half open. Drool glistened on the side of his chin. Ashley aimed her camera inches from his face and pressed the shutter button and then she turned to me and smiled. I gave her the thumbs-up sign.

Oliver stood in the field with his back toward us, his

hands at his crotch, looking down, then up at the herd of fluffy clouds in the deep blue sky.

Catface jumped on my lap and swayed her tail from side to side. Hey you, I said. Before I could start scratching her head she jumped into the backseat and onto Ashley's lap. You have to pee too, Catface? Ashley cooed. She saw me looking at her and then winked at me again. It was confusing me—all her winking.

Oliver trotted back, relieved. Hey, did you know that Gandhi used to drink his own piss?

Eww, Ashley said, her mouth twisted in disgust.

So did John Lennon, I added.

Shut up, Digit, Oliver said.

It's true, man. What do you think that yellow submarine song is all about?

You're full of it.

Whatever, I said. I know what I'm talking about.

Oliver released the hand brake and stepped on the accelerator.

Enrique's eyes fluttered open. He was still out of it and his voice came to us as if from underwater: *Are we there yet?*

8

AW, MAN, WHO FARTED? Oliver wanted to know.

Don't look at me, I said. Enrique?

Wasn't me.

Then we saw the field of cows to our right, stretching out into the horizon. Black cows and beige cows, white cows and spotted cows. The scent of manure filled the Buick like cigarette smoke blown into a beer bottle.

Ashley covered her mouth and nose with one hand. *Gross!*

Oh, Jesus, Enrique moaned.

Roll up the windows, Oliver said.

I lifted my shirt from the collar, covering my face

from the eyes down. I looked at the cows. Some were standing and some were lying down. Some were chewing bales of hay stacked side by side along the fence. The ones that faced the highway and watched us zoom past looked bored. It took a good five, ten minutes before the stench left the car but an hour more before we stopped talking about the cows. Ashley vowed to become a vegetarian. Enrique vowed to eat more hamburgers. Oliver said his uncle in Texas works at a slaughterhouse, that he has to wear goggles and rubber gloves and galoshes because there's so much blood splashing around.

I can't believe how many cows there were, I said.

It was like Lollapalooza for cows, Oliver said. The Flaming Cows were playing.

And Modest Cow, I added.

Sonic Cow.

The Polyphonic Cow.

Cows of the Stone Age.

Yeah, and the Cows, Enrique said.

We all looked at him. Even Oliver turned around for a second. The Cows? he said. That's the best that you could do?

Enrique shrugged.

We drove on in relative silence. There was the soft hum of the engine and the pop of Ashley's bubble gum and the occasional yawn from Enrique. I imagined there was probably a whole mess of other kids out there just like us, who listened to the same music and wore the same faded jeans, kids who drank the same beer, puffed on the occasional joint and laughed in the gray smoke, whose fathers died or beat them up. I looked at the empty field to my right and imagined all those kids standing there, the whole dissatisfied throng, T-shirted and disheveled and angry at the world.

I was there the last time my dad beat Enrique. I was there and saw it coming, how they circled around each other all morning, brooding, the air sizzling with tension.

Are you going to clean your room today? my dad asked from behind the newspaper.

Maybe, Enrique said.

What do you mean *maybe*?

I mean I might clean it or I might not clean it.

Enrique opened the refrigerator and took out the milk.

I think you might want to if you know what's best for you.

Oh, you know what's best for me now?

Watch it, my dad said, peering over the paper.

I was sitting at the kitchen table, eating leftover pancakes from the Pancake House, my heart beating fast.

My Zoloft is what's best for me, Enrique said, uncapping the milk and pouring it into a glass. Without that, I'm screwed. And I wonder why I'm so fucked up.

Don't talk to me that way, my dad said. He put down the newspaper and walked briskly toward Enrique. Who the hell do you think you are, huh?

Enrique opened the fridge and put the milk back and turned around and faced my dad. I'm Enrique Mendoza, he said. I'm fifteen years old. I'm half Argentinean and half Peruvian. I live in Cerritos with my brother, Marcus, my mother, Nora, and my psychotic fath—

My dad's fist landed square on his mouth and Enrique fell backward, slamming against the fridge. He covered his mouth and when he removed it there was blood all over his lips and chin.

A few weeks earlier I'd made a promise to myself that the next time my father hit Enrique I would jump in for a change, I would make him stop. But I stayed out of it like I always did, cutting my pancakes with the side of the fork, wishing I had the guts to do what my mind was screaming: *Stop him. Fuck your pancakes and just stop him.*

Enrique spit blood on the kitchen floor. See, he said, wiping his mouth with the back of his hand. You're psychotic.

My dad raised his fist and punched Enrique on the mouth again. There was a crunching sound like pebbles under a tire. Enrique was on the floor holding his mouth, the blood dripping steadily now onto his shirt. Then my dad lifted his leg and kicked him in the stomach and when I heard Enrique moan, I jumped from the table—yes, finally I did something, finally I put down my fork and scooted back so the chair legs screeched, finally I stood—and lunged at my dad and put him in a headlock. Enrique grabbed his legs and we wrestled him to the floor, grunting, our bodies banging against the cabinets, the dishwasher.

I heard the glass door open and my mom shouting, *What's going on? Stop it, stop it!*

Motherfucker, Enrique growled. I could see the bloody destruction of his mouth, the large gaps in his teeth.

My dad flailed and cursed, an elbow caught me in the ribs, and the pain was an electric current through my body. I tightened my grip around his neck and he squirmed and coughed. My dad was choking and I didn't care. *No mas, Marcus,* he wheezed.

I let go. We all stopped and the only sound was the sound of our collective breathing, of my mother's quiet whimpering in the living room. Enrique rose and stood before the sink and spat blood down the drain. My dad went into his office and banged the door shut. I went to my room and turned on the stereo and sat on my bed, my ribs throbbing where my dad's elbow had stabbed me. We were like repelling magnets that pushed against one another to the corners of the house.

Later on in the afternoon my mom and I crouched down on the kitchen floor and cleaned up the blood with sponges and paper towels. We found two of

Enrique's teeth. They looked like chips of white marble. She put them inside a plastic Baggie and would carry them in her purse when she took Enrique to the dentist the following week, thinking perhaps they could be glued back in place, as if Enrique were a model airplane with a snapped-off landing gear that could be repaired.

That night, Fourth of July fireworks cracked and boomed a few blocks from our house. I watched the horizontal blinds of my bedroom window glowing pink and emerald and blue. Every now and then a bottle rocket whizzed overhead and popped like a cap gun. I allowed myself to cry a little and fell asleep with my cheeks still wet. In the morning, Enrique woke me up.

Asshole's gone, he said. His mouth was swollen and purple with a crimson cut down the bottom lip. He held my dad's handwritten note, the lined piece of paper that read: *I'm leaving. Don't look for me.*

Finally, he was out of our lives.

Or so we thought.

This is wrong, you guys, Oliver said. I think we missed our freeway.

We were driving through a town called Crows Landing, a town—from what we could see from the highway—that was no town at all. Just hills and a high chain-link fence to the west. The hills were blond except where blackened patches from a brushfire swirled through the landscape. It looked like marble cake.

Why's it called Crows Landing? Enrique asked while chomping on some Cheetos. I don't see any crows.

I flattened out the creases of a map of Central California and followed highway 5 with my finger. I glanced over the blue veins of rivers, followed the black veins of roads and freeways. I found many cities—Los Banos, Santa Nella, Gustine, Newman—but no Crows Landing.

Come on, Marcus, Ashley teased. I thought you were our navigator.

Sorry, guys, I said, feeling incompetent.

Do we need to turn around? Enrique wanted to know.

No, I said, my eyes racing around the map. I don't think so.

Oliver sighed. If Nub was Columbus's navigator, we'd all be living in Greenland now.

The backseat erupted with laughter.

Catface began to meow. Someone's hungry, Oliver said.

You think she'll eat some of my Cheetos?

She'll eat anything. She'll eat her tail if you put ketchup on it.

I finally found Crows Landing on the map—way north of the freeway that would take us straight to Monterey. Shit, I said. We need to turn around.

Great, Oliver mumbled.

I knew it, Enrique said.

Ashley held one of the Cheetos up to Catface. She hesitated, then leaned forward and sniffed at the orange treat. Come on, Ashley said.

Catface sneezed and shook her head wildly.

Great, I've got cat snot all over my hand! Ashley held her arm out stiffly as if she were wearing a cast.

Enrique laughed again and I looked at his tongue, orange from the Cheetos. I looked at his perfect teeth. I couldn't even tell that he had caps. The dentist had told us that three were knocked out, not two. We figured the third one must've slid under the refrigerator during the scuffle and was now collecting dust.

Our dad had been gone for almost a week when I found the third tooth. The dark purple bruise around Enrique's mouth was now yellow, as if someone had taken a highlighter to it. My mom was ironing one of her blouses and watching a soap opera, her eyes going back and forth from the screen to the board. Enrique was on the couch, his feet kicked up on the coffee table, and I sat across from him with my sketchbook. He was foreshortened, a tricky angle to draw—his legs were crossed and pointed toward me, his head small beside the bottom of his shoes. The iron hissed. There was melodrama coming from the television, shouting and tears and moody piano music. Enrique yawned and scratched his head. *Stop moving,* I said. *Hurry up already,* he replied. *I'm bored to death.* That's when I saw it, his third tooth, wedged between the treads of his shoe like a piece of white plastic, like a chip of seashell, some fragment washed up on the shore with all the other broken things.

9

WE WERE SEVENTY MILES outside of Monterey when Oliver pulled off the highway and into a gas station. We were surrounded by flatlands and a few anorexic trees and nothing much else. There were dozens of dead bugs on the windshield, tiny winged things reduced to yellow streaks. The air was hot and dry and made my skin feel like cardboard. While Oliver was filling up the gas tank in the Picklewagon, I opened my sketchbook and worked on a drawing I had started the day before: a giant crow perched on a house, the bird's wingspan wider than the roof. Ashley leaned forward between the headrests.

That's cool, Marcus, she said.

Thanks.

How did you learn to draw like that?

I don't know, I said, making hatch marks on the side of the house. Family genes, I guess.

Ashley turned around. Can you draw, babe?

Nope. I didn't get that gene.

Ashley leaned forward again and looked over my shoulder. Hey, can you draw a picture for me?

Sure, I said, my hands getting all clammy. What do you want me to draw?

I want to get another tattoo, she said. When I was a kid I had a dream about this hummingbird. It was blue and green and it was drinking from a flower that was shaped like a heart. Would that be hard to draw?

Ashley's breath smelled like cinnamon bubble gum. I wanted to kiss her. I wanted her to know that I wanted to kiss her.

I could do that, I said.

Cool.

Where do you want the tat? Enrique wanted to know.

My chest. Right over my heart.

Enrique pulled Ashley toward him and started kissing her neck.

Oliver popped his head into the car window. Anyone need to use the bathroom?

Me, I said, and jumped out of the car and into the dry heat.

I had to get away from them. I was liking Ashley more and it was really starting to hurt. I thought about her coming to our house day after day, what that would do to me. I pictured her sitting at our dinner table, the side of her fork sliding through my mother's flan, the perfect shape of her lips as she slipped another sweet bite into her mouth.

The bathroom at the gas station had stall doors painted mint green and on one of them someone had drawn a gigantic penis with a black marker. The balls were two adjoined circles with short lines radiating outward, quick dashes that were supposed to be pubic hair. It looked like a dick stuck on a cactus.

Oliver walked into the bathroom whistling. That's about how big mine is, he said, gesturing toward the vandalized door.

Sure it is, I said. I was wetting my face at the only sink in the bathroom, and the mirror above it was all scratched up with more graffiti—gang names and fuck-yous and a heart skewered on an arrow.

Oliver was pissing in one of the urinals and the back of his T-shirt was damp with sweat. So how long do you think your brother and Ashley are going to last? he said.

I don't know.

I give them a month.

He seems pretty happy with her, I said. For a depressive, I added.

Oliver hit the silver bar on the urinal to flush and zipped up and moved toward the sink. Hey, has your brother ever tried to commit suicide?

No, I said. Not that I know of.

Oliver's hands were under the faucet's column of water, wetting them.

Why, have you ever thought about it? I asked.

No. You?

Nuh-uh.

Oliver shut off the water and yanked out a few paper towels from the chrome dispenser. I wanted to tell you something, he said.

Shoot, I said.

Those pictures.

What pictures?

The ones in the glove compartment. That wasn't my aunt in the photo, he said. He wiped his hands on the paper towels and balled them up and then dropped them into the trash can. That was some woman my dad was screwing and got pregnant.

I leaned against the wall. Does your mom know?

Yeah. She went to the same church that my parents went to.

That's messed up.

I know, Oliver said. My father paid for her abortion. Three days later he hanged himself.

Shit, I said.

Enrique walked into the bathroom with a bounce in his stride. Thought I didn't have to go, he said, and stood before one of the urinals and unzipped. How much farther do we have to go? he asked over his shoulder.

About an hour, I said.

Oliver was quiet and his face was blank like a sheet of paper with two eyes. There was a small cricket on the floor and he watched it crawl across the tile. The cricket moved quickly in one direction, stopped, moved quickly in another direction, stopped again.

And I knew what he was going to do before he even lifted his foot and slammed it down.

A week after my dad left us, the bruise around Enrique's mouth was almost gone when the kid who lived across the street, Chuck Phillips, gave him a new one—a dark purple shiner that made it look like my brother was wearing an eye patch.

We were tossing a Frisbee on the street in front of our house, Enrique and me, the blood-red disc gliding back and forth between us. Since it had only been seven days, I feared our father still might come back and imagined him pulling up into the driveway, standing with us, and snatching the Frisbee in midair.

The Phillipses' garage door opened and Chuck wheeled out on his BMX and came down the driveway, pedaling sluggishly. He rolled around Enrique and said something I couldn't quite make out, something about throwing like a girl. I tossed the disc and Enrique caught it and held it out to Chuck but pulled it away before Chuck could grab it. Chuck got off his bike and let it fall to the street and the front tire spun by itself like a roulette wheel. He snatched the Frisbee from Enrique's hand and pitched it up into the nearest tree. Enrique pushed him in the chest, hard, so his head snapped back. Chuck swung and hit Enrique square in the eye and I ran toward them.

I was going to jump in like I did when my dad was beating Enrique in the kitchen. I was ready to put Chuck in a headlock and everything, but by the time I reached them, Enrique was already pummeling the poor kid, jabbing and kicking and pulling and jabbing. He clutched the back of Chuck's hair and ground his face into the pavement. When Chuck rolled over on his back I could see threads of skin on his forehead, blood streaming from the wound. His nose was crooked and two bloodworms slid out of his nostrils and down his cheeks. Enrique lifted his fist again. I grabbed his arm.

Let go, my brother yelled.

Stop, I said.

Enrique stood and kicked Chuck on the leg and pointed up at the tree. Get it, he said.

What? Chuck said.

Our Frisbee. You threw it up there, now go get it.

Leave him alone, I said.

Chuck coughed and wiped the blood leaking out of his nose onto his shirtsleeve. He looked up into the tree's architecture, the red disc stuck in the middle of it. I can't get up there, man.

Enrique cocked his fist and lurched forward. Chuck flinched.

Okay, okay, he said. Someone's got to give me a boost, though.

Enrique stood by the tree and wove his fingers together and held them at his knees. Come on, he said.

Chuck placed one hand on Enrique's shoulder and stepped onto my brother's locked hands, using them like a stirrup. Enrique lifted him up and Chuck reached for the lowest branch, grunting. A blood drop rolled off his face and disappeared in the grass.

Come on, monkey boy, Enrique said, looking upward with his hand pressed against his brow like a visor. How 'bout a banana, monkey boy? Enrique smiled, and his missing teeth were open windows on a white building.

I realized then who my brother was becoming,

what kind of boy he was backing away from.

You won already, I said. Leave him alone.

Enrique said nothing more. We looked up in silence and watched Chuck Phillips climb higher and higher, leaves spiraling down like ticker tape as his arm stretched out toward the Frisbee, a fat heart caged in the ribs of the tree.

We all pitched in and got a room at a Best Western just outside of Monterey, the bruised sky of dusk hanging over us. Enrique volunteered to approach the hotel manager, to say he lost his ID and that he could pay more if necessary, but it wasn't. The hotel manager was, according to Enrique, the biggest flaming homo that ever walked the earth.

He was practically batting his eyelashes at me, Enrique said. He sat down on one of the two beds in the room and kicked off his Converse sneakers. I think he was wearing blush, he said.

He didn't ask for your ID or anything? Oliver wanted to know.

Yeah, but I told him I lost it at a club. Then he told me how much he loved going to clubs and dancing. I swear, I think he really was wearing blush.

Ashley sat beside Enrique and put her arm around his shoulder. Was he hitting on my boyfriend? she teased.

Fuckin' faggot.

Ashley quickly removed her arm. Don't say that, she said. God, I hate that word.

Which one? Enrique asked. *Fuckin'* or *faggot*?

Ashley stared at Enrique hard. Are you homophobic? Because if you are, I need to know.

I was sitting up on the other bed with my back against the headboard, watching their exchange. Catface yawned and arched her back.

No, I'm not homophobic, Enrique said. I just don't like it when some butt pirate is eyeing my brown eye.

Hey, is anyone hungry? Oliver was sitting at the small round table in the corner of the room, flipping through the Yellow Pages. Should we order some pizza or what?

You can be such a prick sometimes, Enrique. Ashley stood and turned around and sat on the bed opposite my brother, her ass just inches from where I'd stretched out my legs. When she leaned forward, the waist of her skirt opened like a pocket and I could see her panties, a thin strip of pink fabric.

Come on, Enrique, stop drinking the Haterade, Oliver said.

Are you going to order pizza? I asked.

You need to calm down, Enrique said to Ashley, and picked up the remote and turned on the TV.

Yeah. Should I get two larges?

I *am* calm. Don't tell me to calm down.

One pepperoni and one cheese? Oliver held the phone in his hand, the Yellow Pages split open on the table.

I like black olives, Enrique said, clicking through the channels.

You know I don't like olives, Ashley said, annoyed.

Oops, I forgot.

That's passive-aggressive.

Okay, forget the olives, Enrique said. Get whatever, I don't care.

The air between Ashley and Enrique was sour. I always hoped that they'd fight one day, that one fight would lead to another fight that would lead to their breakup, but I never thought I'd witness that first fight.

I tried to contain my excitement.

Ashley tapped the side of my leg with the back of her hand. Scoot over, she said. I did and she sat up beside me, arms crossed, so the side of her right arm touched the side of my left arm.

While Oliver was ordering the pizzas, Catface jumped on Enrique's bed and he pushed her off the mattress with his socked foot. She fumbled to the carpet and meowed and moments later jumped on the other bed where Ashley's and my feet were. She stared at me with her topaz blue eyes and blinked slowly, wondering if I was going to kick her off the bed too.

10

ENRIQUE'S PSYCHIATRIST was in Downey, four flights up a beige building with windows tinted so dark it looked as if the entire structure was filled to the roof with ink. There were six palm trees rising from the sidewalk and a brick path to the front entrance, a heavy wooden door that reminded me of castles and galleons.

Enrique's appointments with Dr. Kumar were every two months, usually a Wednesday, and my mother always drove him and waited in the lobby for his session to end. Always, that is, except for the day she was sick in bed with the flu.

Can you take him, Mijo? she said, coughing.

Do I have a choice? I said.

The lobby at Dr. Kumar's office was a small room with eight cushioned chairs pushed against the walls, four on each side with a glass coffee table in between and magazines fanned out: old issues of *Time*, *Sports Illustrated*, *People*, and *National Geographic*. It looked like any other lobby. There was even an aquarium against a wall with colorful fish that glided from one end of the tank to the other. They were vibrant, striped, quick in the water. One fish was velvet black and had its mouth suction-cupped to the glass. It reminded me of Enrique when he was a kid, how he'd press his mouth to a window and blow, lips smashed, his cheeks ballooning out.

Help yourself to some water if you like, the receptionist said, pointing to the watercooler beside the aquarium.

Thanks, I said.

She smiled and turned back to her computer. She had bleached blond hair, almost white. Her face was pale, her lips colorless. She looked like the ghost of herself.

I stared at the fish for a while, sliding back and

forth, but that got boring really quick so I picked up a *Sports Illustrated* from the bottom of the pile. Buster Douglas was on the cover wearing his fat red boxing gloves and heavyweight title belt. The issue was ancient, from 1990. The cover barely held on to the staples. I was surprised no one had swiped it yet and sold it on eBay.

I thought about Buster Douglas pounding on Mike Tyson, the stunned crowd as Tyson was knocked out, fumbling around for his mouthpiece, dazed by the fists of an underdog.

I never punched anyone, never got into a fistfight, but I often wondered how it would feel. To hit and be hit. To hurt someone who was doing the same to you.

I imagined Enrique in red trunks, my dad in blue trunks, the twelfth and final round. Enrique on the ropes and my dad throwing punches into his mid-section, his own belly spilling over his trunks, love handles jiggling with every jab. Enrique's left eye swollen shut, a deep cut on his brow dripping blood. My dad throws an uppercut and misses and Enrique bobs to the side and throws his own uppercut, landing square on the chin. The crowd gasps as my dad's knees buckle, as he teeters and falls with his arms limp at his side. He slams to the canvas and the referee counts him out, cameras flashing everywhere, the crowd roaring, chanting my brother's name in three syllables: *En-ree-kay, En-ree-kay, En-ree-kay!*

The door to the lobby swung open and a man walked in wearing blue jeans, a sweater, and a baseball cap. He stood at the receptionist's desk with his back toward me as he signed his name on the clipboard. When he turned around I saw that his entire face was scarred, mottled by fire. He had no eyebrows, no hair that I could see under his hat. He picked up a *Time* magazine and sat directly across from me.

I tried not to stare.

Birthday candles, he mumbled.

What?

My face, he said, pointing at it. I was blowing out birthday candles and *whoosh*!

Really?

No, not really. He smiled and his splotchy pink skin stretched over his cheeks.

I felt like a dumbass so I flipped through the *Sports Illustrated* and started reading this article on Jennifer

Capriati. There was a photograph of her fiercely swinging her tennis racket. She'd just turned pro and was only thirteen years old when the issue came out. *Thirteen.* I was four years older and hadn't accomplished squat except graduate from middle school.

I lost money because of that guy, the burned man said.

I looked up from the Capriati article. What guy?

Buster Douglas.

I flipped over the magazine to the cover and looked at Buster's plump face, his dopey smile.

It was a fluke, he said.

What really happened to you? I blurted out.

He closed the *Time* magazine and tossed it on the coffee table. I'm a fireman, he said. Was, I mean.

Oh, I said.

The roof caved and I fell down with it.

The door to Dr. Kumar's office opened and Enrique walked out carrying a brown paper bag. The bag reminded me of the lunches my mom would pack for us, our names felt-tipped across the brown paper. The one my brother carried now was blank. It could've belonged to anyone.

You ready? Enrique said.

I stood up and looked at the burned man. See you later, I said, even though I probably wouldn't.

He nodded and did this quick hand motion, a salute with two fingers against the bill of his baseball cap. It was all backward. I should've been the one saluting him.

In the hallway, Enrique began to snicker.

What's so funny? I asked him.

That guy looked like a circus sideshow.

Don't be a dick, I said.

Am I right or am I right?

I woke up with Oliver's bare feet beside my face. We'd slept on the same bed at the Best Western, our heads on opposite ends of the mattress like the dual profiles of the jack of spades. Quietly I climbed out and looked at Enrique and Ashley on the other bed. They had made up the night before and her arm was now flung across my brother's chest, her green hair splayed on the pillow like the fronds of a palm tree.

In the bathroom I splashed water on my face and brushed my teeth and got dressed. I opened my wallet and pulled out the folded piece of paper that had my dad's address written in my mom's neat handwriting.

There was a knock on the bathroom door.

It's me, Enrique said.

I opened the door and my brother's eyes darted like a hunted animal.

What's wrong?

My meds.

What about them?

I forgot to bring them.

That was smart, I said.

Enrique stepped into the bathroom. He turned on the faucet and cupped his hand underneath and lifted water to his mouth. He splashed water into his hair and raked it back with his fingers.

You'll be okay, I said. You took one before we left yesterday morning, right?

He looked at me and said nothing.

Are you kidding me? I said.

I had other things on my mind.

How do you feel now?

I feel okay, he said, but it'll probably hit me later on this afternoon.

The last time I saw Enrique off his medication, a couple months after Dad left, he was curled up in his bed, facing the wall. He cried for hours, his body quaking underneath the blanket. Afterward, his face went rigid, his temper spiked. He grabbed a lamp and slammed it over and over against his desk until the lightbulb popped inside.

I sat down on the toilet seat. Maybe we should drive home now, I suggested.

No, he said. We're already here.

I don't think it's a good idea, Enrique.

Where's the pistol anyway?

It's in my backpack.

He's probably the reason I still need those pills in the first place, he said.

I stared at the bathtub, the drain and black rubber stopper. I know, I said. Then I started crying like a damn baby.

Hey, my brother said.

I'm sorry I didn't do anything.

It's okay, man.

I should've helped you.

You think you could've stopped him?

I don't know, I said, wiping my eyes with the back of my hand. I should've at least tried.

You jumped on him that last time, he said. Surprised the shit out of me. Usually you just sit there like you're watching a school play.

I chuckled. I cried some more. That bastard, I said, sniffling.

Let's do this, okay?

I stood and went to the sink to wash my face for the second time. I patted myself dry with one of the motel's white towels hanging from the towel rack.

Okay, I said.

They were all inside the Picklewagon waiting for me to get off the phone. Oliver honked the horn and I walked to the window and pulled back the curtain, the phone cord stretching behind me. I raised a finger and mouthed, *One minute.*

Enrique's fine, Mom, I said. I told you already.

Make sure he takes his pills.

I do.

You have to watch him take them. Sometimes he forgets.

I've been watching, I said.

How was the circus? she asked.

We're going tonight, I lied.

Can I talk to Enrique? she asked.

He's in the shower.

Oliver revved the engine and began tapping the horn, making it chirp.

I have to go, I said. Oliver wants to use the phone.

Be good, Mijo, she said.

Once I was outside, Oliver slammed the horn and didn't let go until I was in the car and sitting in the passenger seat. That's funny, I said, my voice flat.

What did she say? Enrique asked.

She just wanted to know if we were enjoying ourselves, that's all.

Some of us are, Oliver said as he pulled out of the parking lot. He readjusted his rearview mirror. Right, Enrique?

What are you talking about? Ashley said.

You didn't hear anything last night? Oliver asked me.

I shook my head.

I'm sure, Ashley said. Like I would do that with you guys there.

It sounded like you did.

Ashley's voice was stern. I was having a nightmare. Enrique, tell them.

We did the hokey pokey all right, he said.

Ashley punched my brother on the arm. You're a pig, you know that?

Catface jumped from the backseat and climbed onto my lap.

Damn, I was kidding, Enrique said, rubbing his arm. She was having a nightmare.

Is that what all that groaning was about? Oliver asked, still unconvinced.

Yes.

What was your nightmare about? I asked.

Ashley leaned forward in her seat. It was really weird, she said. This witch was chasing me all around school. And there was this man hanging from that huge tree by the gym. It was awful. His face was all blue and he was kicking his legs like crazy.

The car grew quiet. It was as if the world was on mute. And then it hit Ashley: Oliver's dad. The cord, the basement.

Oh my God, she said. Oliver, I'm *so* sorry.

It's okay, he said. Where am I going, Nub?

I had the map unfolded on my lap, a black circle marked around the street where my dad lived. Make a left at the next light, I said. We're looking for the Monterey-Salinas Highway.

I completely forgot that—

Ashley, don't sweat it, Oliver interrupted.

There it is, I said. Get in your right lane.

Oliver turned on the blinker and merged over. I rolled down the window and the coastal breeze blew in, smelling of the Pacific. We drove past a vineyard where thousands of sticks were evenly spaced on the dirt with vines coiled around them. We passed a golf course with perfect grass and pine trees out of a textbook, white carts gliding over the green landscape. I saw a man standing in one of the sand traps, one gloved hand on his waist, the other holding his club like a cane. Thinking.

How far away are we? Enrique wanted to know.

I looked down at the map. The black circle I'd made with a Sharpie had bled through to the other side.

Not far at all, I said.

11

MAKE A RIGHT AT the next stop sign, I said.

I'm really looking forward to meeting your father, Ashley said.

I looked at Enrique in the side-view mirror and our eyes met.

Some other time, babe, he said.

Why not today?

You can meet him in a couple weeks. He'll be living with us then.

What? There was a pause. How come you didn't tell me? she asked.

I forgot to.

Another pause.

You're lying to me, Ashley said.

We almost there? Enrique asked.

Yeah, I said. This is the street.

Why are you lying to me?

Stop it, Ash, Enrique snapped. Goddamn.

The car fell silent.

I looked out the passenger-side window. It was a quiet neighborhood with lots of tall trees and houses far away from the curb, their lawns manicured and lush green.

What's the address again? Oliver asked.

It's 771 Belshire, I said. It's an apartment building.

You're acting strange, I heard Ashley whisper to Enrique.

That's it, I said, pointing. The gray building with the balconies.

Oliver parked the Picklewagon three houses away from the building and killed the engine. A woman in red sweats walking her Labrador glared at us suspiciously and then picked up her pace, the dog's nose skimming the sidewalk, sniffing.

So I guess we'll just wait here, Oliver said, meaning him and Ashley.

How long is this going to take? Ashley asked. Her arms were crossed and her eyebrows were furrowed.

Not long, Enrique said.

How long is not long?

I don't know. Ten minutes, a half hour. Just sit tight, okay? Enrique leaned over to kiss her on the cheek, but she backed away, dodging his lips. What the fuck? he said.

Don't talk to me like that.

I wouldn't have to if you'd stop acting like a bitch.

I stepped out of the car and slung my backpack over my shoulder and waited for Enrique, who was still inside the car arguing with Ashley. Oliver looked at me through the windshield and lifted his fists to his cheeks and turned them back and forth. Ashley was crying.

Minutes later Enrique stepped out of the car and slammed the door and walked briskly to where I stood.

Is everything okay? I asked.

Yeah, everything's cool, he said. Come on, let's go.

We walked up the tree-lined sidewalk, both of us quiet. I was nervous as hell and rubbed my sweaty palms on my jeans. Enrique stared at me.

Why are you freaking out? he said. I'm the one he beat.

I'm not freaking out.

What's his apartment number again?

He's in 105, I said. Probably the first floor.

I should clock him, he said. Enrique made a fist and socked the meaty part of his palm. He hadn't taken his pills for two days and now I could tell.

There was a concrete path at the front of the building. It curved through the grass and then split in two directions, forking around the building with smaller paths that branched out, leading to the front door of each apartment. There was a FOR RENT sign stapled to a piece of wood and hammered into the grass. Below the phone number it read: DO NOT DISTURB OCCUPANTS.

This is the wrong way, I said. The apartment numbers are going higher.

We doubled back and went around to the other side. The gray paint and black wrought-iron balconies made the building look more like a penitentiary than anything else. It didn't seem like a place you'd want to visit, let alone call home.

Let me say a few things first, Enrique said.

I might say a few things too.

It's in your backpack, right?

Yeah, I said, patting the bag with my hand.

Vertical blinds clattered open to our right and my heart flinched.

There it is, Enrique said, pointing at a door.

We walked up the narrow path, me in the front and Enrique trailing behind, and I remembered then the rope bridge we crossed at the county fair when we were kids. It might've only been ten or so feet off the ground, but I was scared out of my mind as the wooden planks wobbled underneath my sneakers. At the end of the bridge was a small wooden fort with fake cannons and iron telescopes. There was a pirate flag whipping in the wind, a skull with an eye patch wearing a musketeer's hat. *Go, Marcus,* Enrique shouted from behind. *You chicken shit, go!*

I rang the doorbell and we waited. I let out a deep breath. There was a swarm of butterflies fluttering in my stomach. I stared at the peephole and waited for the little circle of light there to go dark. We waited and waited.

Ring the bell again, Enrique said. And I did.

Nothing.

He must be working, I said.

Enrique cut in front of me and knocked on the door forcefully.

Again, silence.

I was somewhat relieved that he wasn't home, but I also wanted to confront him, to say things to his face that needed to be said.

Let's come back later on, I told Enrique.

Fuck, he muttered.

We turned around and headed back. Where the blinds clattered open there was now a boy at the window, his little hands pressed against the glass. Enrique waved and then the boy was gone and the door to his apartment opened.

The child was barefoot and wore a diaper and a lemon yellow T-shirt with Winnie-the-Pooh on the front, his paw stuck in a jar of honey. *Hi*, the boy chirped.

Nice shirt, I said.

Look what I got, the boy said, and crouched, lifting an action figure off the ground. *Batman!* the boy shouted, and tossed the toy up, somersaulting in the air. When it slammed against the walkway he ran out of the apartment howling, his diaper slipping off of him.

A woman's voice roared from within the apartment. *Alex!* And then she was standing in the doorway, cigarette in hand, her face flushed. *Get back inside here!*

When Alex didn't move she went to the boy and lifted him up by one arm, still holding on to his Batman, also by one arm, so the two of them—the boy and his action figure—looked like monkeys in a barrel.

How many times have I told you not to run out that door? his mom scolded.

We turned away from the two of them and seconds later we heard the door slam and the boy wailing behind it.

That was quick, Ashley said once we were back inside the car.

He wasn't there, Enrique said.

Oliver started the engine. Where to, Nub?

Don't call him that, Ashley said.

It felt good, Ashley sticking up for me. But ten

154

minutes later I heard her and Enrique whispering to each other, then kissing, and it felt like a thumbtack was pushed into my heart.

When I was a freshman I used to play this trick on people with my finger. I'd jam the stub deep into my nostril so it looked as though I were picking my brain. I did this to Christine Walsh in biology class. Christine was the captain of the cheerleading squad, the most popular girl at school, and her parents were filthy rich. On her sixteenth birthday they bought her a convertible Volkswagen Bug. It was cherry red and had a white leather interior. Her license plate read QTGRL4U, which made it sound like she was a hooker or something.

Hey, Christine, I said, my stub already in my nose. *That's disgusting.*

I pulled my finger out. I'm not really digging, see? I said, showing her my little stump.

Oh, she said, her face twisted in confusion.

Omar Ramirez, a slim Mexican boy with crooked teeth, leaned toward me from his seat. She's a snob, he said. She has a maid to wipe her ass.

I laughed.

What happened? Omar asked.

What do you mean?

Your finger.

Oh, I said. That. My pops. I'll tell you about it later.

After class, in the hallway, Omar asked again about my finger and I described an imagined scene. How my dad yanked me by my hair into the garage. How he pulled down my mom's garden shears. How I never felt anything so painful in my life.

Omar's eyes widened with horror. *Jesús Cristo*, he mumbled. While students shuffled around us, while lockers opened and clanged shut, Omar gazed off over my shoulder, stunned by what I'd just told him.

Man, I'm just playing with you, I finally said, smiling.

He punched me on the arm and we were officially friends.

Omar and I hung out during lunch break and after school. At his house we played *ESPN NFL Football* on his PlayStation. We were always the Raiders and after each quarter, we'd pass the controls over to the other.

One afternoon, Omar said to me, You wanna see my dad's gun collection?

I had the controls and right then my quarterback was sacked in the end zone.

Damn it, I said. Sure, why not?

I followed Omar into his father's office. On the desk there was a stack of manila folders, bills lined up evenly in an envelope holder. There was a Swingline stapler, a coffee mug filled with sharpened pencils of equal length, a multicolored rubber-band ball. Omar opened one of the drawers and lifted a tray and took out a small silver key. He went to the mahogany wardrobe in the corner of the office, a junky wooden thing that looked like it had been pulled out of a swamp. He slipped the key into the keyhole and swung open the double doors.

The inside of the wardrobe was another story. It was upholstered in green felt, the kind used on billiard tables. Propped like tools in a shed, from top to bottom, was his father's gun collection: 9mms, .33s, .45s, Glocks, Berettas, Smith & Wessons. You name it and it was there. He even had rifles hanging from the doors, one with a scope. Resting on the bottom of the wardrobe were clips and magazines and boxes of ammunition. Omar opened one of the boxes and took out a bullet.

Feel how heavy these are, he said, placing the bullet in my hand.

I rolled it around my palm for a while and then put it where my finger used to be. Omar laughed. I gave him the bullet back and he slid it inside the box as if it were a silver crayon with the wrapper peeled off.

The following week Omar shot himself in the head, but somehow he survived. They said if he'd tilted the gun a little higher, just a couple more degrees, he would've been dead. The suicide attempt left him drooling in a hospital with tubes snaking out of his arms and nostrils. Some blamed his parents, some said a Marilyn Manson song made him do it.

This happened when I was a sophomore. By the time I was hanging out with Oliver and Britt and Darren the following year, getting wasted and lifting CDs at Tempo Records, I'd almost forgotten about Omar.

Until I got his postcard from Dallas.

On the front of the card was a rodeo clown poking

his head out of a barrel, a black bull charging right at him. On the back, my name and address was neatly printed, but the handwritten note was in a child's scrawl. My name was spelled MARKUS and everything afterward was practically unreadable, as if it were written in a school bus going over a thousand speed bumps. The only sentence I could figure out was this: *When you put finger in nose was funny I remember.*

After we chowed down on some burgers at McDonald's we decided to go to the Monterey Bay Aquarium. We left Catface in the car with some Chicken McNuggets and hoped she wouldn't leave her own nuggets in the car while we were gone. I pushed my backpack with the starter pistol under the front seat. Just to be safe.

Enrique and I had a moment alone while Ashley and Oliver were using the bathroom at the aquarium. When do you want to go back? I asked him.

Tonight, he said. It has to be tonight.

We don't have to do this, you know.

Maybe you don't, but I do.

Okay, I said. Tonight it is.

We checked out the sea otters first and then the penguins. We checked out the indoor tide pool and dipped our hands in the water. We touched starfish, sea anemones, brown turban snails, and hermit crabs.

Pretty, Ashley said, her green hair dangling down the side of her face like kelp.

This is boring, Enrique said. I'm going over here.

We followed him down a corridor and soon we were standing with others in a dark room before a giant wall of blue water. Hundreds of fish glided by: spotted and striped, silver and rainbowed, ones shaped like torpedoes and ones that looked like silver pancakes. A manta ray skimmed the floor of the tank and another hid in the pebbles, his one visible eye slowly blinking. There was a black fish with fat lips pressed to the glass and I thought of the small aquarium at Enrique's psychiatrist's office. I thought of the burned man in the waiting room and how his face resembled the sea turtle that floated past, flapping his arms in slow motion.

For a long time we stood there and didn't move, in silent awe.

A shark emerged from the dark blue shadows of the

water and headed straight toward us, all stealthlike.

Creepy, Oliver said.

I like sharks, Ashley said.

Enrique turned to her. Really?

Yeah. Not the mean ones, though.

They're all mean, Ash.

I looked at Enrique and noticed his jaw tightening. He was clenching his teeth.

No, they're not, Ashley said. Not that shark over there, she said, pointing at one that was spotted like a leopard.

The shark reminded me of my bad acid trip, the one I saw coming out of the bathroom's darkness with all those fins and my dad's face. I remembered how just before then, Ashley winked at me and then someone turned off the lights. I remembered the strong scent of roses. But then I remembered something else, something I never remembered before: a kiss, quick on my mouth. I racked my brain, wondering if it was true or if my mind was playing a trick on me. Or maybe the acid I'd taken had destroyed a part of my brain that stores away memory. As soon as I convinced myself that I'd imagined the kiss, I remembered it again, real as anything.

Hell-o, yoo-hoo, Ashley sang, snapping her fingers by my face.

What? I said, embarrassed.

They were all looking at me. Ashley, Enrique, and Oliver.

Sharks, Ashley said. What do you think of sharks?

I like them. They're cool.

Let's go this way, Enrique said, stepping away from us and through the mob of people.

He's cranky, Ashley said over her shoulder.

We moved through the crowd and found Enrique in another room standing in front of a smaller tank. He was surrounded by a group of excited kids on a field trip, screaming at one another and jumping in place as if they all had to use the bathroom. Their teacher was a tall man in khakis with a white long-sleeve shirt rolled to his elbows.

Inside voice, you guys, he said. The kids' hollering didn't even lower one decibel. He might as well have said, Keep shouting until my ears bleed.

What is it, what is it? one pigtailed girl asked.

It's a monster, a boy roared.

Where's his head?

It's a spider.

Stop pushing me!

Spiders can't swim, retard.

He doesn't have a head.

What's that on his arms?

Mr. Hall, Billy called me a retard!

When Mr. Hall finally calmed his students down and rounded them up in the next room, Enrique stood alone, eyeing the giant octopus. It moved across the water like a strange nightmarish hand. The tentacles waved and curled and arched, its thousand suction cups fastening and unfastening from the glass.

Ashley walked up behind him and placed her hand lightly on his back. Hey, is everything all right? she asked.

Enrique turned around. Yeah, he said weakly.

Oliver was reading a plaque at the base of the tank and I stood by him, giving my brother and Ashley space.

It says here that it has a beak, Oliver said.

No shit, really?

And it changes colors to express emotion.

Weird.

Like a mood ring, Oliver said.

I examined the octopus, the fat, rubbery laces of its arms. They were peach colored and I wondered what that meant, what emotion it was feeling. I thought that if I had to spend my entire life inside a tank, I'd be pretty pissed off. I'd be bright red.

The octopus crawled over the rocky floor of the aquarium. Its alien head bloomed to violet and the color slowly seeped down to each of its tentacles.

I glanced over at Enrique. His back was turned toward me and Ashley's arms were wrapped around him, her head resting against his shoulder. And I could tell by the expression on her face that right then, while the octopus turned completely purple, Enrique had begun to fall apart.

12

WHILE OLIVER WENT TO get us some sandwiches at Subway, Ashley and I sat with Enrique in our room at the Best Western and mulled over what to do with him. He curled up on one of the beds and sobbed. He screamed at us when we tried to convince him it was time to go home. His face scrunched up like a fist. *No*, he shrieked. *We're not going home.* Ashley ran her fingers through his coffee brown hair. It's okay, sweetie, she cooed.

By the time dusk came around and filled the sky with pink clouds, a calmness washed over my brother, and his face then reminded me of our neighbor's, Mr. Murphy, the day an ambulance backed up into his driveway. My dad had always said the Murphys were crazy and that he wouldn't be surprised if they all ended up in the loony bin. Then one Sunday morning the paramedics took Mrs. Murphy out on a stretcher. *See?* my dad said. *What did I tell you?* Later on that afternoon, Enrique and I stood on top of the air-conditioning unit in our backyard and watched Mr. Murphy ride a child's bicycle around and around his swimming pool, his pale face serene as a statue's.

Oliver returned with our sandwiches and set the bags on the table.

Enrique washed himself up in the bathroom. When he came out, he looked at us with his wet hair combed back. I feel better, you guys, he said. Really, I do.

Ashley walked up behind my brother and looped her arms around his waist.

Good, I said. But I still think we should head back home.

It's going to be dark soon. Let's leave first thing in the morning, he suggested.

To San Francisco, Oliver added. We have to see my uncle.

Forget it, I said.

What do you mean *Forget it?*

We need to get my brother home. He's not well, if you haven't noticed.

It's my damn car. Oliver glared at me. And we agreed we'd see my uncle after your stupid little stunt here with Enrique.

What stunt? Ashley said, looking at Enrique. What's he talking about?

Nothing, he said. It's nothing.

I thought you had a whole sheet of your uncle's acid left? I asked.

I do, but he told me he's got some uppers. And some other shit he couldn't mail to me.

Marcus, it's okay, Enrique said. We'll drive to San Francisco in the morning, get the pills, and then we'll head back home.

It'll only take us an hour and a half to get there, Oliver said. Two hours tops.

Catface jumped on the small table in the corner and began licking her forepaws.

Whatever, I said. I leaned back on the bed and kicked off my shoes and let them thump on the ground. Do what you want, I don't care.

Oliver clicked on the television and the four of us watched the sports highlights in silence, then a few lame commercials, then the weather forecast for the Bay Area. Scattered showers in the morning with a chance of thunder, the pudgy weatherman said. On the screen was an animated cartoon cloud with blue raindrops across three frames.

I'm not even sure if the windshield wipers work, Oliver said.

Great, I muttered.

I thought about the afternoon Enrique and I flew a kite in the rain, how we tied a key to the tail and wished for lightning. The kite was black with big yellow eyes like an owl's. The wind pushed it higher and higher into the charcoal gray sky and the wooden handle spun in our hands, vibrating as the string unspooled. The rain pelted us and we watched the kite sway side to side above us like the head of a cobra ready to strike.

Enrique jumped out of bed, full of energy, and picked up my backpack. Let's go, he said.

You've got to be kidding, I said.

We're not leaving Monterey until we see him.

Let's stay here, babe, Ashley said. You've had a rough day.

Oliver didn't take his eyes off the TV. I'm staying here, dude.

Fine. Can I borrow the car?

Sweetie, Ashley said.

Oliver dug inside his front jeans pocket and pulled out the keys. He flung them at Enrique, who caught them with one hand.

Don't go, Ashley pleaded.

I have to, Ash.

No, you don't, I said.

Look, I'm going. Enrique slung the backpack over one shoulder. You can come or you can stay here, I don't care either way.

I looked at my little brother, who was now tall with broad shoulders and whiskers on his chin. Once he was a cheerful kid, giggling on a merry-go-round, in a bathtub with a cloud of suds on his head. Once he shucked off his swim trunks and ran naked along a shore, howling like a car alarm as my dad ran after him, his footsteps sinking deep into the wet sand.

Enrique's hand was on the doorknob. Well? he said.

Wait, I said. Let me put on my shoes.

Ashley pulled on a sweatshirt and flung her green hair over the hood. I'm going too.

It felt strange letting Enrique drive. At home, I was always the one behind the wheel while he sat in the passenger seat, his feet kicked up on the dash. Even though I'm only a year older, I felt fatherly toward Enrique on those drives to the market or the mall or wherever we went, like there were things in life I could teach him. But here in Monterey, more than three hundred miles from home, with Enrique driving and me in the passenger seat, I felt small, like it was his turn to give me the lesson.

We were a few blocks away from the apartment building. I had the map open and the dome light on. We're looking for Charlwood Avenue, I said.

Got it, Enrique said.

You're going too fast.

No, I'm not.

I glanced over at the speedometer, where the needle pointed to sixty. Yes, you are. This is not a freeway.

Slow down, babe, Ashley said from the backseat.

Streetlamps flew past and their orange light slid quickly in and out of the car, pulling our shadows into the windshield.

Slow down, Ashley repeated, almost yelling.

Damn, okay, Enrique snapped. I heard you the first time.

A siren whined far off and I looked behind us. Ashley had also turned around and faced the back window. Oh no, she muttered.

A police car approached us, blue and red lights strobing.

Nice going, I told my brother.

Shit, Enrique said. The *gun*.

A bolt of panic struck the car, jolting all of us.

What? Ashley said. *What gun?*

I grabbed my backpack and shoved it deep under the passenger seat.

It's a starter pistol, actually, Enrique said. It's not loaded.

What the hell are you doing with a starter pistol? Ashley asked. I *knew* something was going on.

Relax, you guys, just relax, I said even though I was

far from being relaxed myself. The gun was under *my* seat—the cop would think it belonged to *me*.

Enrique slowed down and began to pull over. *Damn it*, he shouted, and slammed the heel of his palm against the steering wheel.

Shit, shit, shit, Ashley chanted. We're going to jail.

We're not going to jail.

Yes, we are. If you have a gun—

It's a starter pistol, Enrique yelled.

Okay, everyone calm the hell down, I said. If you don't, he's going to think something's up.

The tires of the Buick crunched over gravel as we rolled to a stop. The police car pulled up right behind us and our skin and hair and clothes flashed blue, red, blue, red.

I glanced over at Ashley. She rocked back and forth, her arms wrapped tightly around her as if she were wearing a straitjacket. I reached over and placed my hand on her knee. We're not going to jail, I said. Nothing's going to happen.

Ashley swallowed hard and placed her hand on top of my own.

Just be calm, everyone, I said, but when I glanced

over at Enrique, he'd begun to weep. Whether it was fear or lack of meds or a combination of both, I couldn't tell.

Get a grip, I snapped at him.

The police officer knocked on the glass. Enrique rolled down the window.

Good evening, the officer said. He shined his flashlight at my brother's face, his wet cheeks. Enrique sniffled and wiped his nose.

What's going on here? the officer asked.

My, my dad, Enrique said, stammering and weeping. He just, my dad, he just died.

The officer shifted the flashlight to my stunned face, then Ashley's, then back to Enrique, who was still muttering on, playing the role of the boy who lost his father.

We're going, we're going to see . . . , he continued. Going to see my mom. He made a fist and held it against his forehead. Oh God, Dad. Why, God, *why* . . .

Enrique leaned in to the steering wheel and a string of snot stretched down from his nose.

I'm sorry, son, the officer said. But you can't drive as fast as you were driving.

I know, I know . . .

What's your name?

Enrique leaned back in his seat. Oliver, he said. I know I was going fast, I'm sorry, my mom called, she was hysterical. Enrique covered his eyes with one hand. Oh, Dad, he mumbled. *Oh, Dad.*

The officer shined the flashlight on my face again. And your name?

I could've peed on myself right then.

Alberto, I said, which is my middle name. I'm his friend, I added.

The flashlight's beam crossed over to Ashley, frozen in the backseat, her mouth half open. Only her eyes moved.

And yours? the officer asked.

Ashley said nothing. Her eyes quickly darted to mine and then back to the officer.

That's Cindy, I said. She's my girlfriend.

Look, the officer said, turning his attention back to Enrique. I can't let you drive in this condition. His tone was soothing, sympathetic.

He's right, Oliver, I said. Let me drive.

Enrique wiped his eyes with his palms. He took a

deep breath and let it out. Okay, he finally said.

My legs felt numb as I stepped out of the car and walked around the front of the Buick, my fingertips trailing the hood. While Enrique was standing by the road, the officer placed his hand on his shoulder as if he were consoling his own son.

Moments later the police officer was nothing more than two red taillights shrinking into the night. We sat in the car for a long time, catching our breath.

I think I'm going to be sick, Ashley said, her voice cracking.

Roll down the window, Enrique offered. He wiped his face with his shirtsleeve and sighed. Jesus, he said. I should get an Oscar for that performance, don't you think?

I leaned back and breathed slowly out of my nose, trying to calm down my heart. I lifted my hands off the steering wheel and they trembled in the orange light of a streetlamp.

Enrique chuckled as if he'd been acting the whole time, but I was right there, sitting right beside him. There was something darker happening to him that went beyond simple role playing.

It's not funny, Enrique, Ashley said. What's wrong with you?

Babe, nothing happened. Why are you so pissed?

Because I told you to slow down.

I stared at my brother hard and shook my head.

What? he said.

We're going back, that's what.

Like hell we are.

I'm not doing this, I said.

Then drive me there and I'll do it myself.

No way.

Come on, Marcus.

I said no.

Screw you, then. Enrique grabbed the map from the dashboard and yanked the backpack out from under the passenger seat.

What are you doing? I said.

Enrique opened the car door.

Sweetie, stop, Ashley said. Please, get back in.

The door was wide open and Enrique already had one foot outside, his body half turned away from us. He looked at me over his shoulder. You're either driving me there or I'm walking there, he said.

Tires shrieked in the distance. A car blared its horn and a man shouted into the night.

Now, my brother said, which one is it going to be?

Enrique and I have stood on many doorsteps together. Like the afternoon our Frisbee sailed over the wall and into the Murphys' backyard. We let Rock Paper Scissors decide who would knock on his door, but when I won Enrique begged me to go with him until I said yes. I made my brother ring the doorbell, but then he cowered behind me. When the door opened, Mr. Murphy was wearing a three-piece suit and a fluorescent yellow diving mask. The Frisbee was already in his hand, balanced on top of his fingertips as if he were some stuffy waiter at a fancy restaurant. I believe this flying contraption belongs to you, he said, his voice all nasal from the mask pinching his nose.

There was also the time we stood on the doorstep of the Chinese family that lived on the corner of our street. We'd heard they were giving away puppies. The door opened and this Asian woman stood before us in black pajamas with cherry blossoms embroidered on the sleeves. Where are the puppies? I asked her. She shook her head and said something in Chinese. *Puppies*, I said. Do you have any *puppies*? When the woman shrugged, Enrique began barking spastically and panting with his tongue out. Then she closed the door in our faces.

There were Halloweens when we went door-to-door together, swinging our bags of candy. One year I was a werewolf and Enrique was Dracula. I complained to my mom that my flimsy mask looked lame, so she spray-painted some cotton balls brown and glued them onto the mask. I was pretty happy with it until Chuck Phillips's dad asked me if I was supposed to be Fozzie Bear. Enrique wore a black vest and a black cape and had plastic fangs that glowed in the dark. My mom painted fake blood on the corners of his mouth that dripped down to his chin. Every time we rang the doorbell, Enrique said, *I vant to sock your blod*. We got our handfuls of candy and then we moved on to the next house, the next welcome mat, and waited for another door to open.

But now we stood outside our dad's apartment, the porch light yellowing our skin, the air ripe with the scent of coming rain. I thought of Enrique's plastic fangs, the teeth my dad would knock out years later. I thought of my brother barking like a dog and the puppies that didn't exist, their invisible whimpers. And as Enrique readjusted the backpack over his shoulder, I thought of Mr. Murphy answering the door in his diving mask, the strangeness of that moment, as if the world were a dream in some other boy's head.

Enrique rang the doorbell and took a step back.

I stared at the circle of light in the peephole and rubbed my palms on my jeans.

Footsteps thudded behind the door like a heartbeat through a stethoscope.

The peephole went completely dark.

There was a long pause.

Then the door opened.

13

MY DAD WAS IN PAJAMA bottoms, a wife-beater shirt, and blue slippers. The last time I saw him his belly was out to here, huge, but now it was half the size. His hair was all messy as if a strong wind had been blowing inside his apartment. Black and gray whiskers bristled along his cheeks and chin. He looked old. It was as if we hadn't seen him in ten years instead of just one.

What a wonderful surprise, he said. He held his arms out, but when he saw that neither Enrique nor I wanted to give him a hug, he put his arms down and stopped grinning. Come in, come in, he said, opening the door wider.

The living room was small and immediately made me feel claustrophobic, like if I turned around too quickly I'd knock over a lamp. There was a brown leather couch for two up against the wall with a framed painting of geese flying above it. On the wood-chipped coffee table was a fake potted fern, a bowl of empty peanut shells, *TV Guide*, and two remotes. A family photo sat on a doily, the one taken at Sears with the sunset backdrop and silhouetted palm trees—I looked like a dork with my banana yellow shirt buttoned up all the way to my throat. In the corner of the room, a small television was angled on top of a dresser and the gray screen reflected the entire living room in miniature.

I had no idea you guys were coming, my dad said. Your mother didn't tell me anything.

We wanted to surprise you, Enrique said.

That you did! My dad put his hands on his waist, then down at his sides, then on his waist again. I can't believe you're here, he said, beaming.

I didn't know what to say. Looking at his scruffy appearance, the new life he'd created for himself, I felt kind of sorry for him.

It's good to see you, Pops, I finally said, which wasn't entirely true. A part of me—a big part—wished we hadn't driven up here in the first place. I would've been much happier spending the last two weeks of summer in Cerritos, hanging out with Oliver and Britt and getting wasted. But there was also this part of me that wanted answers from my dad, to understand why he always beat Enrique and never me, to hear him say that he was sorry.

Sit down, my dad said, motioning toward the couch. Can I get you guys anything to drink? You want some peanuts?

I sidestepped the coffee table and sat down at the end of the couch. I'm fine, I said.

Enrique sat beside me and dropped the backpack between his feet.

Enrique? my dad said, pointing at him.

No, thanks.

Are you sure?

Yes, I'm sure.

Let me get a chair.

My father walked into the kitchen, his slippers skimming the linoleum and making that *tsk-tsk* sound that slippers make. The kitchen, from what I could make of it from the couch, was about half the size of the living room. Just enough space for a refrigerator, small table, wooden chair, and nothing else. He opened the fridge and peered inside for a while and then closed it. He grabbed the back of the chair and carried it into the living room and sat down.

So, how are you two doing? he said.

We're doing okay, I said.

Enrique nodded.

Are you still drawing, Marcus?

Yeah.

Good, good, he said. You're going to be a famous artist one day.

Enrique picked up *TV Guide* and thumbed through the thin pages.

School starts again soon, doesn't it? my dad asked.

In a couple weeks, I said.

Enrique turned the backpack over so the zipper was at the edge of the couch cushion where he could easily reach it.

You're going to be a senior, right?

Right, I said.

He turned to Enrique. And you're going—

A junior, Enrique said, cutting him off.

My dad smirked and shook his head from side to side. I can't believe how fast you two have grown, he said. He lifted his hands and clapped the top of his thighs. Are you sure I can't get you guys anything to drink? he asked. A Coke? Some orange juice?

I'm sure, Enrique said.

I'm fine, Pops, I said.

My dad smiled. It was hard for me to believe that this was the same person who did the things that he did. He looked like a man full of regret, the way his face slouched, the sadness behind his smile. We came here expecting to find the same dad that left us, a man who filled a room with his body and voice, who could make his own son bleed, but the person sitting before us was not that man.

I had to stop Enrique.

On second thought, I said, orange juice sounds good.

My dad clapped his thighs again and stood and went to the kitchen.

I leaned in to Enrique. Don't do it, I whispered. It's not right.

I knew you would puss out on me, he whispered back. You were always a pussy.

You're off your meds, I said. You're not thinking straight.

He knocked my damn teeth out.

I reached for the backpack and Enrique clasped my forearm tightly with his right hand. If you fuck this up, I will fuck you up. Enrique glared at me, his jaws clenched. You hear me? he whispered.

I yanked my arm away from him and leaned back on the couch. For a moment the imprint of his fingers was there on my arm, white on pink, then disappeared into the butterscotch of my flesh.

My dad came back from the kitchen holding a tall glass of orange juice and set it before me on the coffee table.

Thanks, Pops, I said. I lifted the glass to my lips and drank.

He sat back down on the chair, huffing. So, Enrique, my dad began. Your mother tells me that you have a girlfriend now.

Yep.

Allie, is it?

Ashley.

Right, right, *Ashley*, my dad said. That's a pretty name.

Yes, it is.

How long have you two been together?

She's in the car, Enrique said.

Oh, my dad said, frowning. Why didn't you invite her in? My dad turned to me, confused, then back to Enrique. I thought you guys would be here for a while. I thought we could catch up.

You thought wrong, Enrique said.

I set the glass of orange juice down on the coffee table. Dad, I said.

What is it?

I looked at the bowl of empty peanut shells and imagined my father breaking them open, twisting them in his hands. I looked at Enrique, his profile, the little muscle twitching along his jaw line.

I know, I know, my dad said, shaking his head slowly, side to side. What I did was wrong. And I apologize, to both of you. I should've never abandoned you guys the way I did.

Enrique chuckled and looked down at the backpack.

What? my dad said.

You don't get it, do you? Enrique said. That wasn't the problem. We were *glad* you left. We were never so damn happy, to be honest.

He leaned forward in his chair. Now, Son, I know I wasn't the best father to you.

To say the least, Enrique shot back.

I'm sorry, I'm truly sorry.

I know you are, Dad, I said.

Enrique put his hand up in front of my face. Don't, he said. Just stay out of it.

What's going on here? my dad wanted to know.

What are you sorry about? Enrique asked him.

My dad opened his mouth, but nothing came out.

Tell me, Enrique said, his voice rising. What *exactly* are you sorry about?

My dad bowed his head and wove his fingers together and said something under his breath.

What's that?

Hitting you, he mumbled.

Louder.

Hitting you, he repeated. I'm sorry I ever hit you, Enrique. I was wrong and—

Are you sorry for *all* the times you beat me?
Enrique said.

Yes, of course.

Like the time I went over a rock with the lawn mower?

Yes, Son.

And the time I scratched up the ceiling with the ladder?

Yes.

How about when you kicked me in the leg after I spilled juice on your goddamn sofa chair?

Yes.

And when I tracked mud into the house and got it all over the carpet?

Yes.

I was barely nine years old, Enrique said. *Nine*, he yelled.

My dad fell silent. I could hear the clock on the wall behind him, softly breaking the seconds.

How about the time I came home late from a party and you punched me in the stomach and then pushed my face in my own vomit? Are you sorry you did that?

Yes, Son.

And the time I accidentally broke the aquarium in the living room?

Yes.

How about this? Enrique said. He opened his mouth and ran the tip of his forefinger along his bottom teeth. These here are fake, he said. You knocked the real ones out.

My dad dropped his face into his hands. He stayed like that for a while and then he glanced up at Enrique. I'm sorry, Son, he said. Please, let me make it up to you.

Oh, yeah? And how are you going to do that? Enrique reached down and unzipped the backpack.

Stop, I said.

Stay out of this, Marcus, he yelled. The cords in his neck stood out and his face bloomed red.

Enrique, please, stop screaming, my dad said.

How are you going to make it up to me? Enrique asked again. How?

As soon as I move back into the house, I'll show—

Move back into the house? Enrique said, jerking his head back. You're not moving back into the house. I just told you we were happy you left.

But I haven't been, Enrique. It's been very difficult for me not having you two in my life.

Boo fuckin' hoo.

My dad rubbed his hands together. He sighed. Look, he said. I've changed, I'm different now.

I can tell, Pops, I said. What I couldn't tell was how long the change would last.

Oh, you've changed, have you? Enrique said.

I'm not who I was a year ago. I went and got some help, he said. A psychiatrist, like we did for you.

Enrique started clapping sarcastically. Bravo, he said. Bravo, Dad. He went and got some help. *Brav-o*.

I've been treated, Son. I don't have those urges anymore.

Enrique stopped clapping. What kind of urges would that be?

My dad said nothing. He leaned back in his chair and folded his hands on his lap and closed his eyes.

What urges? Enrique repeated.

Violent, he said.

Really? They're gone now?

My dad opened his eyes. Yes, Enrique.

Soon after you left, I beat the shit out of Chuck

Phillips, Enrique said. Didn't I, Marcus?

I nodded.

You should've seen me, Dad. You would've been proud. His face was like ground beef after I was through with him. Enrique looked at me and slapped my thigh. Isn't that right?

I nodded again.

Hey, Marcus, remember that day when Scott Duval came to school with two black eyes?

Yeah, I said. I remember.

He looked like a panda bear, didn't he?

I said nothing.

That was me, Enrique said. He turned to my dad. I did that to him. In junior high, he sat behind me in history class. He liked to smack the back of my head for no reason. I'd be writing notes or taking a quiz or whatever and then *bam*, he'd smack me. So, I guess you can call it payback, his two black eyes. But I had to wait until I was bigger than him. Smart move, don't you think?

My dad kept quiet.

I took a sip of my orange juice and set it down. We should probably go, I said.

Say, Dad, do you think I'm bigger than you now?

My dad glanced over at Enrique. You've grown, Son. Both of you have.

I know, but do you think I'm *bigger*?

He glanced over at Enrique once more and rubbed his chin. Perhaps, he said.

You know, I'm not sure that I am, Enrique said. He studied his chest and arms, stretching them out before him. He turned both of his hands—palms up, palms down. Nope, I'm definitely not bigger, he said. Good thing I brought this with me.

Then he reached into the backpack and pulled out the gun.

My dad lifted up both of his hands and leaned back in his chair, startled. His body stiffened. Enrique, he said. What are you doing?

What do you think I'm doing? Enrique said.

My dad's face went completely pale. Put down the gun, he said.

Fuck you.

Please, Son.

Don't call me Son.

Enrique stood up from the couch and I stood with

him. Okay, you've made your point, I said.

No, Marcus, I haven't. Enrique stepped around the coffee table and kept the gun leveled, pointed directly at my dad's face.

Don't do this, he said.

Are you afraid? Enrique asked.

My dad swallowed hard. He looked as if he was about to choke on his own fear.

Answer me.

Enrique, don't.

Are you afraid?

Yes, my dad said. *I'm afraid, yes.*

Good. You should be.

Come on, Enrique, I said.

Let me ask you something, Dad, Enrique continued. Did you think it was fair?

What are you talking about?

The beatings.

No, it wasn't fair.

I mean, I was just a kid. I didn't really have a chance, you know?

I'm sorry.

I was only this tall the first time. Enrique held his

193

left hand out just below his shoulder.

My dad's chin began to quiver.

I had no chance whatsoever, Enrique said.

I moved toward my brother from behind and gently placed my hand on his shoulder. He spun around quickly and his elbow jabbed me on the cheekbone. I dropped to the carpet. Pain sparked inside my skull and bloomed white. I turned over on my side and looked up at my brother, at the gun in his hand pointed between my dad's eyes.

This is going to be messy, Enrique said.

Enrique, please stop, my dad said, his hands still up by his face, his eyes squeezed shut.

Anything you want to say before I pull the trigger?

Enrique, no.

I was lying there on the living room floor, the pain still pulsing in my skull like a heart, when I finally opened my mouth: It's a starter pistol.

Shut up, Enrique yelled.

Dad, it's a starter pistol, I said, standing up. It doesn't even have bullets.

Yes, it does.

He's lying.

Marcus, *shut* the fuck *up*!

My dad looked at me and I saw the terror slowly vanish from his face. He lowered his hands and his body relaxed, settling into his chair.

It's loaded, Enrique shrieked, the gun still pointed at his head.

But it was too late: My dad believed me. Whatever power Enrique had held over him was now gone. I saw it in my brother's face, his trembling mouth.

My dad stood up and casually took the gun out of his hand as if Enrique were passing him a television remote. Enrique's arms dropped to his sides, his chest caved. When my dad tried to hug him, he lifted his hands and pushed. *Get off me*, he shouted.

I forgive you, my dad said.

Enrique shook his head in disbelief.

I moved around the couch and opened the door and walked out.

I'd heard and seen enough.

14

WE LEFT THE BEST Western early the next morning. The first drops of rain hit the windshield and smacked against the roof of the Buick like someone on a typewriter. Everyone was quiet as we headed out to San Francisco to see Oliver's uncle, to pick up some uppers and whatever else he had for him.

I pulled down the sun visor and leaned into the little rectangular mirror there to get a closer look at where Enrique caught me with an elbow, my cheekbone swollen and purple like a plum. I touched the bruise gently and imagined my hands around my brother's throat, squeezing.

The rain came down harder and the wipers went

back and forth across the windshield. Catface meowed in the backseat. Oliver asked me if we were heading in the right direction and I just nodded. I wasn't in the mood to talk.

Everyone in the car said as little as possible. We all, to some degree, hated one another.

The land around us was beige and lonely and the highway cut right through it. We came around a bend and we were surrounded by hills, and up along their backs there were windmills, hundreds of them—an army of white propellers whirling in the rain.

I was looking up at one of them, watching the giant blades turn sluggishly as if it were coming to a stop, when Oliver slammed on the brakes.

Up ahead there was a gray plume of smoke rising from a flipped-over truck, the windshield shattered into a mosaic of glass. On the shoulder of the highway there was a jackknifed horse trailer, silver and dented like a beer can.

Oh my God, Ashley said.

Oliver stopped the car and we all stepped out onto the road. I jogged toward the truck, where the driver was upside down and still seatbelted in. Enrique kneeled down and knocked on the driver-side window. The driver turned toward us, his forehead bloodied. He fumbled for the car door and slowly jerked open the cracked window.

Are you okay? I asked.

Ayúdame, the man said.

Oliver crouched and turned onto his back and reached up inside the car, struggling to release the seatbelt. Damn thing, he said. It's *stuck.*

¿Necesitas un cuchillo? the man asked. His forehead was slashed with bits of glass stuck in it and the blood leaked into his hair.

Do you need a knife? I shouted.

No, I got it. There, Oliver said, and scooted out of the truck.

The man's head was bent and his shoulders rested against the roof of the truck. Enrique and I reached in and pulled him gently out of the car like a newborn.

¿Qué pasó? I asked the man.

Un camión, he said. *Él entró en mi vereda.*

What's he saying? Oliver asked.

He said another truck went into his lane.

Mi caballo, the man said, sitting up and looking at

the ruined trailer. *Mi caballo.*

The rain came down fast and loud, soaking our clothes and flattening our hair against our foreheads.

The man rose and staggered over toward the trailer by the roadside and we followed him. Ashley was already standing there, her arms folded across her chest.

The man's horse was vanilla white and spotted with tan freckles. One of his hindquarters was twisted grotesquely where a bone poked through the skin. Blood seeped out of the wound and down his ruined leg and dripped into the muddy earth. The horse snorted and twitched and whinnied, his eyes big as Ping-Pong balls.

A guttural sound came out of the man's throat and he began to weep, his hand over his mouth. *Ay, Dios mío,* he said. *Mi caballo lindo.*

We stood there beside the man with the rain pelting us and looked down at the horse, the horror in his eyes.

Traffic backed up on both lanes. A woman in a BMW looked on with her mouth half open while a child in the backseat made squiggles on the fogged-up window with his fingertip. A man on a cell phone stepped out of his car and ran toward us, the rain darkening his shirt. The police are on the way, he said. Is anyone hurt?

He is, Oliver said, pointing to the man stumbling over to his ruined truck. He got on his hands and knees and reached up into the smashed-out window on the passenger side. He unlatched the glove compartment and all its contents dropped onto the roof of the truck. Then he was coming toward us through the downpour, carrying a gun and mumbling something in Spanish.

What the hell? Enrique said.

The man on the cell phone turned around and hurried back to his car, his shoes splashing on the highway. He'd already done all he was capable of doing.

The horse grunted and the rain spattered against his body. The man crouched down with his gun and rubbed the horse's neck.

I can't watch this, Ashley said, and walked back to our car.

We stood there—me, Enrique, and Oliver—and watched the man consoling his animal. There was only one option and the man held it in his hand. It was a Colt .45, long-barreled and steel blue.

Lo siento, he said, and stood up and pointed the revolver at the horse's head.

Enrique turned away. Oliver turned away. I didn't.

Lo siento, the man said again.

The horse groaned and it sounded like there was thunder inside him. There was a long pause and it seemed as if I could count the raindrops if I wanted to.

The man lowered the gun and covered his eyes with his hand. *No puedo*, he said.

Enrique turned around, then Oliver.

Por favor, the man said, *alguno de ustedes*.

What did he say? Oliver asked.

He wants one of us to do it, Enrique said.

The man cried and grabbed the revolver by the barrel and held it toward us. *Yo no puedo*, he said.

The horse snorted loudly, his body shuddered and flinched.

Por favor, the man said. *Mi caballo está sufriendo.*

Enrique turned and walked toward our car with his hands shoved deep in his pockets.

The man held the revolver out for Oliver, who folded his arms and took a step back. No way, uh-uh, he said.

The man held the gun toward me. *Le pido,* he said, weeping.

I took the revolver from him and the man pulled the hammer back for me. *En la cabeza,* he said, and tapped his forehead with his middle finger. *Aquí,* he said, and then walked away. His legs buckled under him and he hit the pavement. The woman in the BMW jumped out of her car. She held her umbrella over the man while another motorist rolled up his jacket and placed it under his head. Oliver turned away and headed back to the Buick.

I was alone with the horse. The rain came down and the puddles splashed around me in a thousand little explosions and the horse grunted and shook violently, his eyes wild and helpless.

I looked at the revolver in my hand and saw that my nubby finger wouldn't reach around the trigger. I thought of the brick that severed it, how seconds before Enrique was sitting cross-legged on the grass as I pedaled toward the ramp. I thought how soon after I lost my finger my dad beat Enrique for the first time.

I switched the revolver over to my left hand and it felt strange holding the gun that way, like I was using someone else's hand, someone else's fingers.

I aimed between the horse's eyes. If I had known a prayer I would've said it then, but it wouldn't have mattered anyway. We were two different animals. The horse understood things like field and hay, sunlight and sky. Not mercy.

I pulled the trigger and the gun blast threw me down onto the wet pavement. My ears buzzed and rang like feedback from a guitar and were still ringing when the police arrived and kept on ringing all the way home.

15

MY DAD CALLED MY mom soon after Enrique and I left his apartment and told her everything that happened. When Oliver dropped us off the next day late in the afternoon and we walked into the house, she went off. *What were you two thinking? You lied to me. You said you were going to Las Vegas. I can't believe you would do such a thing. Where in the hell did you get the gun? Marcus, what happened to your face? I didn't raise you two to behave like animals. How can I ever trust you again? Marcus, go put some ice on your face.*

I went into the kitchen and opened the freezer and packed a Ziploc bag with some ice cubes. Then I went upstairs into my room and closed the door and lay on the bed with the bag of ice pressed to my cheek. I thought about the horse. I thought about my dad and Enrique and the horse again, always the horse, broken and shaking in the rain.

Even though I was exhausted from the trip, I couldn't fall asleep. I stayed up past midnight watching the green numbers of my digital clock.

I woke up late the next morning with a headache pulsing between my eyes. I shook some aspirin out of a bottle and swallowed it with a handful of water. Enrique was already awake and eating cereal at the dinner table, the spoon chiming against the bowl. There was a large cardboard box on the table and I heard something moving inside it.

Mom found it in the backyard, Enrique muttered, milk dripping from his bottom lip.

I inched toward the table until I saw the black feathers. A crow's ebony head popped over the edge of the box and swiveled in my direction.

Where did she find it?

I don't know. Ask her.

My mom walked in from the garage carrying a basket of laundry. Marcus, your face looks terrible, she said. Go put some ice on it.

I did already.

It still looks really swollen.

I'll do it again later.

She put down the laundry basket and walked toward the table. Did you see the crow?

Yeah. Where was it?

It was just sitting there in the grass. I've been feeding it oatmeal.

Crows eat meat, Mom.

They're scavengers, Enrique said. They'll eat anything.

I went into the kitchen and opened the fridge. I took out the salami, unpeeled a few flimsy slices from the bag and went back to the table. I held the salami up to the crow. When it opened its beak, I dropped it in.

Is it male or female? I asked my mom.

Not sure.

I think it's male.

You're probably right, she said.

Let's have crow tonight for dinner, Enrique suggested.

My mom scrunched up her face. Enrique, that's disgusting.

I looked at the crow. He sure is quiet for a noisy bird, I said.

He hasn't made a sound all morning, my mom said. I think he's scared.

How come he can't fly?

I don't know. His wings look fine to me.

I leaned into the box and the crow backed into the corner, his claws scratching against the cardboard. He just squatted there silently and stared up at us, his shiny black eyes like drops of ink.

Two weeks later school started again at Cerritos High. I was now in my final year and could stand on Senior Hill next to the courtyard and not worry that some lineman on the varsity football team would slap the back of my neck. It was a tradition at the school—the hard smack that left welts on some unsuspecting kid's neck, branding him as he scurried down the hill.

That first Monday it seemed like everyone on campus looked at me differently thanks to Britt's big mouth. *I heard you shot a horse*, a junior said to me by the lockers. *Is it true you shot a horse?* a freshman asked in the cafeteria.

Yeah, I did, I told the freshman.

Cool.

No, it wasn't cool.

Oh, okay, he said, and walked away with his tray of spaghetti and meatballs.

I was hanging out with Oliver on Senior Hill when he told me about Catface, how sometimes she bolts across the room as if a firecracker went off under her. That cat's psycho, Oliver said.

Did you give her any acid?

No, man.

I stared at Oliver, trying to sniff out the lie on his face.

I swear, he said. She freaks out on her own.

So your mom is cool with you keeping her?

I guess. She likes to jump on her bed in the middle of the night. Scares the shit out of her.

I laughed and imagined Catface in Mrs. Thompson's bedroom, moving quietly across the carpet. I imagined her leaping onto the bed and Mrs. Thompson jerking awake. I wondered if there were ever times when she thought it was her husband, climbing back to bed after getting a drink of water or taking a piss.

Hey, Killer, Britt yelled from behind.

I turned around and saw him walking up the hill, pointing his finger at me like a gun.

Don't be a dipshit, I said.

Would you rather I call you Nub or Freak Show?

Yes, I would.

Okay, Freak Show.

Hey, did you get this flyer? Oliver said. He reached into his backpack and pulled out a fluorescent green sheet of paper and handed it to Britt. I had already seen the flyer, the collage of beer cans and women in bathing suits, a house address scrawled at the bottom in a gangster font.

Whose party is this? Britt wanted to know.

Tower's.

Last time I saw that dude, he was carrying you into the bathroom at the Travelodge.

I was pretty wasted that night, Oliver said, and smiled, reminiscing.

We all were, I said.

Britt socked me lightly on the arm. Especially you, Nub.

I'm never taking that shit again, I said.

Too bad you guys didn't make it to San Francisco.

Yeah, Oliver said, and stared at the grass as if there was something to see there.

I looked over across the courtyard and saw Enrique leaning against a wall with the Heavy Metalers, a crowd I hadn't seen him mingle with before. They had long straight hair, and their attire was simple: black jeans or gray corduroys with a band T-shirt, Tool or Korn or Godsmack. I saw Ashley, her hair now dyed blue, walk up shyly to Enrique. My brother said a few words to her and she turned away and walked by herself across the courtyard. One of the Heavy Metalers shook his head no and his long hair stirred on his back like a curtain that's just been closed.

I waited until Enrique saw me staring at him and I waved him over. He walked leisurely toward the hill as if he was bored with the idea of movement. After we returned from our trip, he went back on his meds and his mood had stabilized somewhat. A week later he had an appointment with Dr. Kumar, who wanted to try out another antidepressant. He seemed to be doing much better. Of course, he still wanted nothing to do with our dad and was content with the idea of never speaking to him again.

My mom, on the other hand, thought I should and kept nagging me to call him, so one Sunday afternoon while Enrique was out mowing the lawn I did. I parted the blinds with two fingers and watched him push the mower across our yard, cutting the grass in neat, even stripes. It was a brief conversation that left me confused: I wanted my dad in my life and I didn't want him in my life. I'd like to see you again soon, he said. Both of you, he added. I watched Enrique make another pass across the lawn. I have to go, I said. Good-bye, Dad.

What's up? Enrique said when he was finally standing beside us on Senior Hill.

Don't hang out with those guys, I said.

Why not?

Just don't.

Whatever, he said.

Bruce Powell, one of the bigger linebackers on the varsity team, snuck up behind Enrique with his hand raised, his eyes focused on the back of my brother's neck. I pulled Enrique behind me and held my hand up at Bruce. Don't ever touch my brother, I said.

Chill, Bruce said, backing off.

You shouldn't be up here, Oliver said to my brother. Someone's going to get you eventually.

Enrique shrugged. Hey, what's that? he said, pointing at the green flyer in Britt's hand. A party?

Yeah, Britt said. Are we going to this thing or what?

Enrique and I looked at each other. It's up to you, he said.

Both of us, I corrected him.

I'd decided to take an art class that year. My teacher, Ms. Elliot, was a short woman with glasses and hair like steel wool. On the first day of class, she had us grab one of the magazines she'd put out on her desk and told us to find an image we thought was striking and draw it. I grabbed a *National Geographic* and found a photo of a boy in the Amazon jungle with a blowgun to his lips. He was bare-chested with red paint on his face. The blowgun was angled up toward the trees. According to the caption, a white-bellied spider monkey was perched high up on a branch. The caption didn't say whether the boy hit the monkey with his dart, but I wanted to believe that he did, that his aim was perfect and the monkey squeaked and fell and the boy now felt like a man.

When all the students pinned up their drawings on the board that Wednesday morning, Ms. Elliot pointed at mine and said, Who drew this?

I raised my hand.

It's wonderful, she said, and leaned in close to my Amazon warrior boy. She straightened her glasses on her nose. Nicely done, she said.

After class I bumped into Ashley in the hallway. We hadn't really spoken to each other since we got back from our trip. I could tell she was glum. She wasn't wearing her little silver stud in her nose and her bright blue hair hung limp to her shoulders.

Hey, you, I said.

Hi, Marcus.

How've you been?

Your brother's an asshole.

He's going through a lot right now, I said. Some heavy stuff, you know?

Yeah, well, she said, and her voice trailed off into the clamor of students moving around us, their small talk and gossip and laughter. I still had some feelings for Ashley, but it was different now—its color and shape had changed. I guess I was going through a lot of heavy stuff myself.

Someone from behind me covered my eyes and their hands smelled of strawberry lotion. It was a game—Guess who? But I knew immediately.

Hi, Beth, I said.

She removed her hands and clicked her tongue. You're no fun, she said, and slapped me playfully on the shoulder.

Sorry, I said. I'll guess wrong the next time.

What makes you think there's going to be a next time? Beth smiled a big flirtatious smile.

Ashley looked at her watch. I have to get to class, you guys. It's all the way over by the science building.

I'll catch you later, Beth said.

See ya, I said, and watched Ashley head down the hallway with the crush of students, a bright blue head in a sea of blondes and brunettes.

I turned to Beth. She was wearing a green sweater that brightened the contrast of her olive eyes. Your brother broke her heart, she said.

I know, I said. He tends to do that.

How 'bout you?

I've been meaning to call you, I said.

Sure you have.

Seriously.

Uh-huh.

I'll call you tonight, I said. Okay?

She shifted her books from one side of her arms to the other. I'll be holding my breath, she said, smiling.

The crow stayed with us for three weeks. We kept him inside the cardboard box and placed him by the TV in the living room. Sometimes during dinner we moved the box to the chair where my dad used to sit and fed him scraps of whatever we were eating: salami, cheese, ground beef from Mom's empanadas, pizza, tuna, fries, and fish sticks. He really loved fish sticks. Some days we took the crow outside and let him hop around in the grass. We were puzzled as to why he didn't just fly away.

What's wrong with him? Enrique said. We were standing in the backyard, looking down at the crow, his feathers blue-black in the bright sun.

I don't know, I said.

He jabbed at the grass with his beak, looking for a worm.

He doesn't fly or talk or anything, Enrique said.

Maybe he's a mute crow, I said.

But how come he doesn't fly?

Who knows? Maybe he's afraid to fly.

That's stupid, Enrique said.

My mom was at the other end of the yard, watering the flower beds. She moved the hose from side to side and the water came out of it like a sheer curtain. She stopped moving her arm and just stood there holding the hose without blinking. It was as if the water had hypnotized her.

Mom, I yelled.

She snapped out of it and looked at me and suddenly the crow leaped into the air, his feathers rustling by my ears. He angled up and flew toward our neighbor's house and perched on the roof. Seconds later he sailed back down onto the lawn.

He's going to leave, my mom said.

I'm tired of him anyway, Enrique said.

I moved slowly toward the crow and reached out

with my hand, palm up. He blinked his oily black eyes and crouched low and lifted off into the air again, flying back to the top of our neighbor's roof. He began to caw, over and over, and it sounded like the rusty hinge on an old gate swinging in the wind.

Hey, he can talk, my mom said. She was looking up at the crow with her hand like an awning over her eyes, shielding the sun.

I wonder what he's saying, I said.

He's saying, *So long, suckers*, Enrique said.

Then he lifted off and flew away from us—a black hole that slid across the sky and over the quiet houses—and I knew that he wasn't ever coming back.